CROCODILE SHOES II

Also available

*Crocodile Shoes – From the North East
to the Wild West*

CROCODILE SHOES II

From Tennessee to Tyneside

Based on the TV serial
created and written by

Jimmy Nail

Adapted by Andrew Crofts

POCKET
B O O K S

New York London Toronto Sydney Tokyo Singapore

First published in Great Britain by Pocket Books, 1996
An imprint of Simon & Schuster Ltd
A Viacom Company

Simon & Schuster Ltd
West Garden Place
Kendal Street
London W2 2AQ

Simon & Schuster of Australia Pty Ltd
Sydney

A CIP catalogue record for this book is available from the
British Library

ISBN 0-671-85586-7

Typeset in Melior 11/12 by
Palimpsest Book Production Limited, Polmont, Stirlingshire
Printed and bound in Great Britain by
Caledonian International Book Manufacturing, Glasgow

07215110

CHAPTER ONE

All their dreams came true. Just when it looked as if it was never going to happen, as if all the wheeling and dealing, the hustling and hyping was going to lead to nowhere, a chink of light appeared in Jed's future and 'Calling Out Your Name' began to get radio airplays. Once light finds its way into a black space there is no containing it: it simply spreads. Once the public had heard his voice they wanted more and the months spent in the studio, not to mention the years Jed had spent scribbling and creating, all became worthwhile because the album was ready and waiting to feed the public's appetite. And when you have an album full of original material you are ready to take a show onto the road, and the great moneymaking bandwagon can get underway for real.

Jed Shepperd became an enormous star because the punters loved what he had to say and the way he said it. He was able to sell out extra nights at Wembley Arena and still have people being turned away at the gates. They even liked the way he looked, and their admiration fuelled his self-confidence. The man who had once seemed so gawky and ill-at-ease in his great shambling frame now appeared trim, fit and in control, even when standing up in front of ten thousand fans. He had become a star. Suddenly he was able to do anything and everything he wanted.

Jed was willing to admit that the level of their success was as much Adrian's achievement as his. No matter how much he might disapprove of his manager's ethics and personal habits, he had to admit that Ade had always believed in him as an artist and had steered him through the jungle of the music business to the giddy heights which he now enjoyed. That didn't make Ade's unreliability any less annoying or his character weaknesses any less despicable, but Jed had still come to think of Ade as a mate, albeit a mate who might not stick by him through thick and thin. He was also grateful to have someone with a vested interest in his success who was willing to handle the vast amounts of contractual and financial paperwork that seemed to have fallen out of the sky onto them, leaving him free to dream his dreams, strum his guitar and search his head for more songs.

Most of Jed's time, when he wasn't touring or performing, was spent in Wiltshire at Studley House. To Jed the whole place had an unreal feel to it, more like a film set than a home. If a location scout for a period drama had been out looking for the archetypal English country house, they could not have come up with anything more perfect than Studley. Its handsome brick walls and leaded windows rose from mature gardens which, in turn, gave way to rolling fields in which sheep grazed as they had done for centuries. It seemed, when Ade had first shown it to him, to be the perfect place to escape from the madness of the world outside in order to concentrate on the next album.

They had turned the study into a mobile studio, equipping it with every sort of guitar and electric piano a self-respecting rock star could want. But that afternoon, with the sun glittering on the swimming pool outside the windows, Jed had been unable to resist the temptation and had run a cable out to the loungers beside the blue waters where Joe, who had worked at the house man and boy for over sixty years, was lazily watering the shrubs with a hose. Jed was strumming on a Fender Telecaster, which was connected to amps inside the studio. Even the lightest strum on the strings boomed magnificently from indoors.

He ran over some chord sequences for a track he was intending to call 'Country Boy', and, as the song developed, he picked up a remote control and pointed it at the house, pressing for a playback. Although he still couldn't resist playing with the technology that his new wealth had brought him, his battered old acoustic guitar still lay within hand's reach on a lounger nearby, like a growing child's almost discarded comforter. He was so lost in his own thoughts and chords that he didn't realise Roxanne had come out of the house until he felt her cool shadow fall across him.

'Hiya.' He said smiling, pleased to be interrupted.

'It's from your record company.' She passed him a bundle of faxes. 'They want to know how the album's coming along.'

'They should be asking Adrian that kind of thing.' Jed felt a twinge of annoyance. The very sight of paperwork made him faintly nauseous. 'He's the manager.'

'But he's not here.' Roxanne was merely stating the obvious, but her no-nonsense, German accent made it sound almost like a rebuke.

'I know that!' Jed let his anger show, knowing she would not take offence. 'He should've been here a week ago! God knows what he's up to. Have you tried the London office?'

'Yes. Seven messages, but none of them returned.' She gestured towards the faxes. 'They ask for an immediate response, Jed. What would you like me to tell them?'

'Tell them . . .' Jed racked his brain to think of an appropriate response but found nothing. 'Tell them Adrian's not here!' To cover his embarrassment at his inability to cope with the situation, he threw down the faxes, grabbed his guitar and headed towards the house, muttering to himself. 'He really should be here to deal with this kind of stuff. Let me get on with writing the songs. That's why we bought this place, for God's sake. I don't know what the hell I pay him for.' He wanted to say something to Roxanne to show he wasn't cross with her. 'Has he called yet?' he asked, turning round.

'I just said – no.' She felt sorry for him in his confusion.

4

'I'll murder him!' Jed shouted and disappeared into the studio to escape her pitying look.

Roxanne was a good personal assistant. She knew when to stay out of the way and she knew when to make comforting cups of tea. She waited a while, until she could hear, from the few bars of 'Country Boy' being repeated over and over, that he had calmed down, before taking in a very large mug.

'Have my Sunday papers arrived from Newcastle yet?' he asked, desperate for something to distract him from the snail-like progress of his work, something familiar and comforting.

'I'm afraid not,' she said. He looked so crestfallen that she just wanted to take him in her arms and cuddle him. 'I could get them faxed through,' she suggested, 'or you could read them off the Net.'

'The *Evening Chronicle* on the Internet? I doubt it, pet.'

'Let me try, at least.'

'Nah,' he said after a moment's thought. 'It's not the same. It's . . .' He couldn't think how to describe the satisfying feeling of turning pages of newsprint, so he mimed the action instead: 'It's just not the same.'

'They were apparently mailed out on Monday.'

'It's Thursday now. By the time they get it here it'll be Sunday and then we'll have to start all over again!' He sank his head in his hands.

Roxanne felt desperate, as if she had let him down personally. 'I struck out again, huh?'

'Roxanne,' he said, pulling himself together,

suddenly aware that he was making her feel bad, 'you are the best personal assistant I've ever had.' She smiled in relief. 'Mind you, you're also the first.' He sipped his tea and looked at her, wanting to keep her standing there a bit longer. 'Tell me something. How come a German girl gets a name like Roxanne? Doesn't sound very traditional to me.'

'They named me after the song. You know?'

'Christ!' Jed was shocked. 'Is it that old?'

'So' – Roxanne spoke quickly to stop him dwelling on the age difference between them – 'is there anything your "first and best" PA can get for you? Anything you need?'

He thought for a moment. 'I need a break,' he decided, grabbing his tea and making for the wall safe. Punching in the combination, he opened the door. Inside were his passport, some papers and an emergency cash float, a couple of one-thousand-pound bundles made up of crisp new fifty-pound notes. He took one of the bundles out, peeled off half a dozen fifties and returned the depleted bundle to the safe, stuffing the money into his pocket.

Still carrying the mug of tea he left the house and made his way to the stable block where a variety of brand-new vehicles were parked for his convenience. He gazed at the silver Porsche, black Jaguar XJ300, red Jeep rag-top and green Triumph 900 motorcycle, glanced up at the sky to check there were no clouds, and decided on the Jeep. Climbing in, he headed off down the gravelled drive. As he approached the metal gates he hit the remote control and they swung slowly open. He drove through and out onto the open road. As the gates swung shut behind him a couple of second-division snappers, slow off the mark, ran into the road and raised their cameras. By the time they had focused Jed had disappeared.

Studley was little more than a hamlet, slumbering picturesquely among the Wiltshire woodlands. Jed parked the Jeep next to some bicycles and walked to the Merlin Inn. Outside an incongruous sign announced: VINYL MART – ONE DAY ONLY! Jed went inside and found the normally stuffy function room buzzing with vinyl collectors of all types. Some were obviously professional DJ's, others were long-hairs, record buffs and fans, mixed up with a few local kids filling an otherwise empty afternoon. Assistants mingled unobtrusively with customers as Jed made his way, keeping his head down and catching no one's eye, to one of the stands and started flipping through the albums.

On the other side of the stand a pretty woman in her late twenties found an album she liked and held it excitedly up to the assistant. 'The Reverend Gary Davis at the Lamp Glass Club in Bedlington?' she exclaimed. 'Is this for real?' Jed thought he could detect a Northern accent in her clear, well-spoken tones.

'What?' The owner spoke through a mouthful of popcorn. 'D'you think somebody dreamed up a title like that just for fun?'

'I used to go to that club!'

7

'No kiddin'.' The man appeared completely uninterested. 'Good for you.'

'How much are you asking for this?'

'Three hundred.'

'Three hundred pounds!' The girl looked aghast. 'The Reverend Gary Davis?'

'He's very collectable now. I think it's 'cause he's blind or something.'

'Blind? Since when did that make for a price hike?'

'Hey, lady, please!' The man had haggled enough. 'Life's too short, you know what I'm saying? Just make me an offer.'

'Fifty pounds?' she suggested.

'Fifty quid?' He winced. 'Go on, then. For a peaceful life.' She handed over the fifty-pound note and walked off with her purchase. 'You're heartless, you know that?' the man called after her, but she just nodded and smiled.

Jed watched as she came to rest at another stand. He liked the way she was dressed, a casual nineties, hippy-chic, very well put together. He mooched across and flipped through a neighbouring pile of albums.

'I used to go to that club,' he said casually, making her look up, 'the Lamp Glass.'

She examined his face. 'I know you, don't I?'

'A lot of people think they know me,' he said, 'but yeah, probably.'

'Jed Shepperd.' She seemed flustered. 'Blimey! What are you doing here, making a video or something?'

Jed shook his head. 'Trying to write songs, so's

I can make another one of these.' He held up an album.

'Right. How's it going?' Jed sighed. 'That good, eh?' She laughed.

'I can't tell you how lovely it is to hear a voice from up home. Do you fancy a cup of tea and a sticky bun?'

'Ooh, yes please.'

They headed through to the rear patio where tables and chairs had been laid out for people to drink coffee and tea. Settling at a table, they ordered. The girl introduced herself as Wendy. 'So what are you doing down here?' Jed asked.

'This is my business.' She handed him a card. 'I work the markets around the world, buying and selling. You occasionally find a gem.' She held up the Reverend Gary Davis album triumphantly. 'Like this. But it's mostly just rehashed teen collections, scratched to bits and played to hell.'

Jed studied her card:

GOLDEN GROOVES
Rare Phonographic Recordings
Wendy Cunningham
PO Box 199
Newcastle-upon-Tyne

'It's a dirty job,' he teased, 'but someone's gotta do it.'

'It beats working in Woollies, I suppose.'

'There's no phone number.' Jed indicated the card.

'I work from home — everything's mail-order.

Saves me having to talk to the weird ones.' She gave a few panting breaths to indicate what she meant. Jed nodded.

'Where are you based, Wendy?'

'Tynemouth. I've got a little place overlooking the sea. It's really lovely. Not that I get to spend much time there. How often do you get home?'

'Not as often as I'd like. It's funny, when I was up in Newcastle there was this great industrial landscape outside my bedroom window. It was easy to write about getting away. Now I *am* away, and I look out of the window here and see the swimming pool, and after the pool I see the beautifully manicured gardens, and after the gardens I see sheep grazing in the fields, and beyond that the horizon.'

Involuntarily, his mind pictured a woman and child, as he wondered how they – the wife and kid he'd lost to a gas-fitter's carelessness – would be enjoying the luxury he now took for granted.

'Great view.'

Wendy Cunningham's words snapped him back to the here and now.

'The best that money can buy. But it doesn't work. I can't write a bloody thing just now.'

'Maybe you need to go home.'

'Oh, yes. I can just see me living back up there!'

'Not living there, just going back to recharge the creative batteries.'

Jed pondered for a moment, picturing all the people he could see if he went home. 'It's not a bad idea,' he admitted, 'but I haven't got time. I've got too much to do. I'm so far behind.'

'This'll be your second album, won't it?'

'Second album syndrome.' He nodded. 'Got to prove the first one wasn't down to luck. This one's gonna show if I have the legs . . . or not. That's why I'm down here.' He waved towards the record stalls. 'I pad around the big house and the gardens all day, looking for inspiration, but all I ever see is sheep!'

'You might just be holding what you're looking for in your hands.' She indicated the albums. He looked down and crossed his fingers. They chatted on as naturally as old friends until Wendy caught sight of her watch. 'I'd better get going.'

'Oh.' Jed felt a stab of disappointment. 'Do you have to?'

'I promised I'd meet the friend I'm staying with. She lives not far from here. She'd worry if I didn't show up.'

Jed nodded and waved for the bill. One of the sales assistants mooched over. Jed opened his wallet and selected one of the gold cards from inside. He passed it to the assistant, along with the albums he had chosen. 'Stick everything on that, would you?'

'No problem.' The assistant carried everything off.

'Would you like to have dinner one night?' Jed asked, hopefully.

'I like to have dinner every night,' she teased.

'No, I meant—'

She laughed. 'I know what you meant. I'd love to.'

Jed smiled in relief. He felt very comfortable

11

with Wendy's sense of humour. It must be something to do with their shared roots. 'How about tonight, up at Posh Hall?'

'OK,' Wendy agreed, 'as long as I'll not be stopping you getting on with the work.'

'Even creative geniuses have to stop for a bite to eat.' He jotted down his address and phone number on a napkin, which Wendy slipped into her purse. 'Eight o'clock all right?'

'I'll be there,' she promised.

'I can send a car for you, if you like.'

'No, thank you.' She shook her head and walked away. Jed watched her go. It was a pretty sight. He was woken from his reverie by the assistant returning.

'There seems to be a problem with your card, Mr Shepperd.'

'Does there?' Jed was startled. He never bothered to find out what state his credit cards were in – someone else took care of all that. He just knew that they always worked, whatever he wanted to buy. It was unnerving to have the system suddenly fail. For a few seconds he couldn't think what to do. He took the card back and remembered the cash in his pocket. 'Take it out of that.' He handed over a fifty-pound note and the assistant disappeared again. 'Bloody plastic,' Jed muttered, staring at the offending item as if trying to shame it into working. He was going to have a lot of things to say to Ade when he eventually turned up.

The moment she was out of Jed's sight, Wendy

was unable to contain herself. She headed straight for the nearest payphone and rang her friend. 'Allison,' she squealed happily, 'you'll never guess who I've just met – and who I'm gonna have dinner with!'

In her excitement she didn't notice the man passing by, or feel his hand as it slid into her bag and removed her purse.

The man kept walking until he was round the corner and then expertly emptied the contents out, sifting through for anything he could use. The napkin with Jed's number on it floated down into a puddle, the writing vanishing in the mud.

By the time Jed got back to the house his Sunday papers had arrived, but somehow he was no longer interested, being more eager to hear the records he had bought. It was only once he was in the studio that he realised he had a problem.

'All this bloody equipment' – he looked helplessly at Roxanne – 'and we haven't got a turntable?'

'They're kind of . . .' – Roxanne searched for the right English word – 'defunct. I'll go out and buy one right now.' She headed for the door.

'Where? Round here?' Jed never ceased to be amazed by the way people like Roxanne rushed to do his bidding all the time. 'Oh, and would you check up on my credit cards? I was knocked back this afternoon. Computer problem or something. Rather embarrassing, for a man of my stature!'

'Really?' She was obviously surprised. 'I'll get on to it.'

Jed had only just had time to pick up his Telecaster and strum a few chords when the doorbell went. 'Yes!' He felt a surge of anticipation. 'Wendy. Here we go.' He stumbled in his haste to reach the video entryphone, his guitar still in his hand. 'Hello?' he said, in the sexiest voice he could muster. But the picture on the screen was of two men in suits, one of whom pushed his ID card up to the camera.

'Mr Shepperd?' he asked.

'Er, yes.'

'I'm Detective Sergeant Calder of Wiltshire police. The Met have asked us to contact you.'

'The Met? What about?'

'They want to talk to you about a Mr Adrian Lynn, your ex-partner in First Ade Management.'

'*Ex*-partner?' Jed couldn't make out what the man was talking about, 'What do you—'

'He's dead, Mr Shepperd.'

Jed let go of the guitar and as the neck hit the ground a massive chord reverberated all round the house.

CHAPTER TWO

T he media moved just as fast as the police and by the time Jed went through the gates in the Porsche, following the unmarked police car, the usual brace of photographers had been joined by a small mob, their cameras' motor-winds whirring as Jed shot past. His face was expressionless as he tried to take in what he had just been told. Ade's body had turned up in the harbour in London, fished out by police frogmen, bloated and distorted from the water and minus an arm. Jed felt dazed and confused, too numb even to be able to feel grief yet for his lost friend.

As the Porsche disappeared down the road the snappers abandoned the entryphone, which they had been hammering for the last hour, and leapt into their own cars to give chase. A few moments later, as calm once more descended on Studley House, a cab came round the corner and drew up. Wendy, all dressed up and ready for her date, stepped out, paid off the driver and buzzed the house.

Inside, Roxanne had been left holding the fort. She was in shock and nervous at the constant ringing from the phones and the doorbell. Jed's only instruction to her before leaving the house was to talk to no one. 'Hello?' She pressed the button and was relieved to see that the pack of photographers and reporters had disappeared off the screen.

'Hi,' Wendy said, guessing she was being watched by the camera. 'Is Jed there, please?'

'No,' Roxanne snapped, 'go away.'

'No . . .' Wendy had anticipated that it might not be that easy to get in to the house of a rock star. 'I'm not a fan. Well, I am, actually, but . . .'

'I've told you' – Roxanne didn't want to talk to anyone – 'Jed's not here. Now please go away!'

Wendy pressed the bell again, determined not to give up. 'But I'm supposed to be having dinner with him tonight! Only I couldn't ring to confirm because my bag was stolen, and it had his number in it . . . hello? Hello!' Roxanne had switched off the entryphone and gone to answer a ringing phone. Wendy looked around for her taxi, but everything at the gates of Studley House was silent.

More representatives of the media were waiting at the police station as Jed followed Calder's car into the compound. As he made his way to the door the flashes popped and motors hummed. 'Give us a smile, Jed,' a cheery voice called out, but Jed only scowled back.

Inside, he was shown into the harsh, glaring light of an interview room where a poker-faced Detective Inspector McClusky was waiting for him. They sat on opposite sides of the table with a cassette recorder in between them. 'Mr Lynn had not been robbed,' McClusky was explaining. 'He had over three hundred pounds in cash on him when he was pulled out of the water, as well as numerous credit cards.'

'So?' Jed felt very uncomfortable being in a police station, even when he hadn't done anything. It was something instinctive.

'So . . .' said McClusky. He obviously didn't like dealing with uppity pop stars any more than Jed liked being there. 'We have a bit of a grey area. Here was a man who had every reason to live. A man who'd suddenly become very successful, primarily by managing you, who had a known weakness for alcohol and drugs, yet was found dead in the Thames having taken neither.'

'And that's grey, is it?' The pace of the interview was making Jed want to scream with frustration.

'Very grey. But they're doing their level best to clean it up, so I'm told. Why do you think someone would want to kill Mr Lynn?'

'I can't imagine why anyone would want to kill anybody. But it's common knowledge that Adrian had a few enemies.'

'Is it?' McClusky seemed to be staring. 'I'm told that you and he used to argue a lot.'

Jed shrugged. 'Do you and your colleagues never have a cross word?'

'Not allowed to do them on duty.' Jed looked puzzled by this. 'Crosswords. So,' McClusky continued, deciding not to push the failed jest any further, 'he had a lot of enemies, did he?'

'It seems pretty obvious that he had one, doesn't it, since he's dead?'

McClusky ignored Jed's increasing irritation. 'So who felt strongly enough about Adrian Lynn that they'd have him knocked off?'

'I don't know.'

'You just said he had a lot of enemies.' McClusky glanced at his notebook for a second as if thinking. 'As far as I can see, Mr Shepperd, the only person who'd be seen to profit from Mr Lynn's passing is his business partner. You.'

'What?' For the first time Jed realised why he had been brought in – he was a suspect.

'You are a shareholder in' – he read from his notes again – 'First Ade Management, are you not?'

'Yes – a minority shareholder.'

'Now that Mr Lynn is dead, you are the *majority* shareholder, are you not? In fact, you will now own one hundred per cent of the company. The whole lot.'

'So what? It was all my money anyway.'

'Oh,' McClusky said, smiling almost triumphantly, 'really?'

'You know what I mean. Look, we were onto a good thing, Adrian and me, making money while having a good time. Why on earth would I want to put a stop to that?'

'Greed, Mr Shepperd. Avarice. I see it every day.'

'You're looking at the wrong guy, pal.'

'I'm not your pal, Mr Shepperd.'

Jed looked at him and realised that that was definitely true. He stood up. 'Right. Am I free to go? Or do I call my lawyer?'

'You're free to go, Mr Shepperd, for the time being. Just let us know where you'll be.'

'I'll be burying a friend,' Jed snapped, as he made his way to the door.

The congregation was packed with the music business, a sea of Ray-Bans and Armani suits. Ade's relative longevity in the business was borne out by the number of bands from his past who had shown up, along with their managers, lawyers and A & R people. There was also a clutch of Ade's former girlfriends sitting together, looking like a bunch of models gossiping backstage. They all fell silent as Jed started to sing, accompanied only by the church organist.

The nights are long since you went away.
I think about you through the day,
My buddy. My buddy. No buddy quite
    so true.
I miss your voice, the touch of your hand.
I wonder if I'll ever understand,
My buddy. My buddy. Your buddy misses
    you.

As Jed stopped, tears in his eyes, a terrible still-ness settled over everyone as they each brooded on their own mortality and the suddenness with which their lucky lives could end.

'Yo, Jed!' a single voice called out, breaking the spell. Jed made his way back to his seat in the front row next to Roxanne. A few seats away Alan Clarke was there to represent the record company. Across the aisle a beautiful woman sat, dry-eyed but looking strained. Towards the rear of the church a hard-faced man in a business suit was staring coldly at Jed, as if trying to memorise every line on his unhappy, craggy face.

The minister came to the lectern. 'Though I did not know Adrian personally,' he said, 'it is evident by your presence here today that he was a popular and well-loved man. Never have I seen this chapel so full of so very many sad faces . . .'

A smooth-looking guy with too much hair for his age tapped Jed on the shoulder. 'Who's looking after you now, Jed?' he whispered.

'I'm sorry?' Jed couldn't believe what he was hearing. Even Ade wouldn't have stooped to this.

'If you need a hand with anything . . .' He passed over his card, which Jed scrunched up and threw to the ground.

'This is his funeral, man!'

'Yeah,' the man said, 'but you're very much alive, son.' Having made his pitch, he turned away and Jed decided to leave it.

Detective Inspector McClusky was waiting outside the church, along with numerous television crews, watching as they all came out.

'Nice service,' Alan Clarke commented.

'I suppose,' Jed said with a shrug, 'if you buy all that nonsense.'

'I realise it's too early to talk about the future, Jed,' Clarke said, 'not the time nor the place. But I just want you to know that you've got the full support of the company. Everyone's right behind you, whoever you decide is going to be looking after you.'

'Right. Thanks.' He looked over to the woman who had been sitting across the aisle and was now talking to some mourners.

'Lucy,' Alan said, following his gaze, 'Adrian's sister.'

'I didn't know he had a sister.'

'Ex-model,' Clarke smirked, 'with a brain. Now there's a rare thing. She works for Warner's as an orchestral contractor. String-fixer to you and me. Books all the fiddlers.'

Jed walked round the crowd until he was beside her and then waited until she was alone. 'Lucy?'

'Hello, Jed,' she said.

'I never knew Adrian had a sister. Anybody else?'

She shook her head. 'Just me.'

'Have you heard anything from the police?'

'I spoke to him' – she nodded towards McClusky – 'earlier on. He seems to think it was either accidental death—'

'That's crap!' Jed exploded.

'—or it was you.'

Jed spluttered for a moment, not sure what to say, unable to work out what Lucy was thinking behind her tragic, cool eyes. 'For what it's worth, Jed, I don't buy either of those suggestions. Not for one minute.'

'Right now,' Jed assured her, gratefully, 'it's worth a lot.'

All eyes turned as a Mercedes 600 Pullman limousine drew up and a distinguished-looking man stepped out. He was wearing a Gandhi-style suit and white shirt, and a whisper of recognition went through the crowd. He walked straight to Lucy and embraced her.

'Lucy,' he said, obviously aware of the impact his arrival had made.

'Warren.' Lucy seemed pleased to see him. 'Thanks for coming.'

'I'm really sorry I'm late. I came straight from Heathrow. Got here as soon as I could.'

'Do you know Jed Shepperd?' Lucy asked. 'Jed, Warren Bowles.'

'Hi, Jed.' Warren extended his hand and they shook.

'Hello there,' Jed responded. 'Were you a friend of Adrian's?'

'Way back when, in the long ago, I was Ade's assistant. Totally useless, I was. He used to send me out to get a drink and I'd come back about three days later with a tape of some band in Manchester!' He smiled self-deprecatingly. 'He could hear a song, though. I mean, really hear it. Sad he couldn't avoid all this.' He gestured around at some of the casualties of the music business in the crowd: old men fighting to stay young and babes with Chanel bags. Everyone was watching Warren with Jed and trying to pretend that they weren't. 'Who's taking care of you now, Jed?'

'No one at the moment. I had a few offers earlier on.' He raised an eyebrow. 'But I decided to pass.'

22

'Bit of advice,' Bowles said magnanimously, 'don't sign anything, or agree anything verbally with anyone. Just make sure you're covered legally.'

The advice seemed sound, if a bit obvious, and kindly meant. 'I'll leave you to it,' Jed said to Lucy. 'I'm sorry we had to meet under such awful circumstances.'

'Could we get together at some point, Jed?' Lucy asked. 'I have some stuff of Adrian's that I'd like you to look through.'

'I've probably already gone through it. The police had me ID all of the office stuff and what have you.'

'This stuff didn't go to the police. It's been with me since just before . . .' Lucy tailed off, unable to complete her sentence. Bowles appeared a little surprised by her words.

'Of course,' Jed assured her. 'Shall I ring you in a couple of days, after all this has calmed down?'

'That would be great.'

As Jed said his goodbyes and left them together, Alan Clarke rejoined him and they made their way to their car under McClusky's beady eye. 'Blimey!' Alan was obviously impressed. 'Warren Bowles! The one and only. The legend.'

'What does he do?' Jed asked.

'You never quite know with Warren. Bit of the Cap'n Bob about him. He used to have his own label. Got lucky with a couple of bands, then sold out. For lots and lots, apparently. You want to go for a beer or something?'

'Thanks, Alan, but I want to get going. I'm going to head up to Newcastle for a few days. Got some things to sort out in my head.'

'Fishing, mate. Try a spot of fishing, if you want to chill out. Good for the head.'

'I might just do that.' Jed looked back at the church. 'I'm going to miss the little bastard.'

As Clarke and Jed drove off, Warren Bowles was putting his arm around Lucy's shoulders. The strain of the day was finally getting to her and she was on the verge of cracking. Over her head he caught the eye of a man who had been standing some distance away, and nodded towards Roxanne. Understanding the instruction, Connors walked over to Roxanne, whose expression darkened as she saw him coming. She stepped away from the people she was talking to.

'What?' she asked, coldly.

'Mr Bowles wants a word.' Roxanne looked across at Bowles and started towards him. Connors grabbed her arm in a painful grip. 'Not here, silly,' he hissed.

Bowles was waiting for her a few hours later at his regular table in his regular restaurant. 'Roxanne!' He stood to greet her as she approached, still dressed in funeral black. 'How the devil are you?' He went to embrace her but she pushed him away. Other diners watched with interest and a waiter stood, holding Roxanne's chair back for her. Bowles smiled. 'Now, now,' he said quietly, 'you don't want your daddy getting to know about

all those naughty things you used to do, do you?'
He went to embrace her again and she stayed still,
frozen to the spot, until he had finished. 'That's
better. Now sit down.'

'Listen, Warren,' she said as soon as they were
sitting, 'I don't want to be mixed up in whatever
it is you're doing. I like Jed.'

'I just want you to tell me about what's been
happening down at the house. That's all.' He
switched his smile to the waiter. 'Can we have
the menu please?'

CHAPTER THREE

Things had changed a great deal since he'd last come home. The address he had for his sister, Emma, turned out to be a detached house on an upmarket executive housing estate, a far cry from the shabby little house she'd been in when he went away. A brand new BMW 735 stood in the driveway as Jed drew up in the Porsche. A group of children, attracted by the car, became even more excited when they saw who was driving it. The legend had come home and they swarmed for his autograph. Having given them what they wanted he went to the front door and knocked. Four-year-old Beckie opened it and stared at him with no flicker of expression.

'Hello, pet!' Jed covered his nervousness with some avuncular jollity, holding out a Harrods teddy bear. 'Remember me?'

'I've got one of them,' Beckie announced, and then shouted over her shoulder, 'Mam! Uncle Jed's here.' Her duty done, she ran off, leaving the bear for Jed to pick up.

Emma came out to hug him and led him through to the kitchen where Beckie had disappeared to. The first thing he noticed was the fridge door. Newspaper cuttings following his recent adventures were attached to the metal with magnets. Everything was on display from his leaving Studley House flanked by the detectives to the funeral with Lucy and Warren Bowles and leaving Paddington Green nick after being questioned by McClusky.

'Arrested in Wiltshire.' Emma looked at him disapprovingly. 'Eeh, Jed!'

'That wasn't an arrest,' he protested, 'just a photo opportunity, courtesy of the police.'

'Poor Adrian, eh?'

'You've got me well covered.' He gestured at the fridge.

'You're big news round here,' Emma said.

'Big news everywhere,' he joked, 'thank you very much.'

'Haven't they got anything better to do?'

'Obviously not.' Something about her mouth caught his attention, 'What's wrong with your lip?'

She put her hand up to cover it and looked edgy. 'It's just a cold sore.'

Jed was about to ask more when Pep came in. Emma jumped from her seat and Beckie wandered out of the room. Emma's fiancée looked very different from the nervy little man on the make that Jed remembered. He still appeared driven by adrenalin, but now he was wearing a sharp suit, a gold Rolex and an air of self-confidence.

'Well y'bugger!' Jed exclaimed. 'Best-dressed tallyman in the town!'

Pep obviously didn't appreciate the send-up,

however gentle. 'Hello, Jed.' He nodded curtly. 'How are you?'

'Fair to middlin'. You're doing famously, by the looks of things.'

'Not as famously as you. Sorry to hear about your manager snuffing it.' He turned to Emma. 'Where's those papers I left on the table?'

'I moved them.' She seemed nervous of him. 'I'll get them.'

'Did I see Omo and Big Chrissie out at the Pelaw cemetery as I drove past?' Jed asked as Emma scurried out of the room.

'Aye. Got themselves sorted,' said Pep.

'Gravedigging?'

'It's a job. And you know what they say about graveyards, don't you? People are—'

'—dying to get in there.' Jed delivered his punchline for him. 'I know.'

'They're actually about to go into business for themselves.'

'What, freelance gravedigging?'

'Some sort of mail-order thing.'

Emma came back in with his papers and Jed noticed him giving her a withering look. 'How long are you up for?' Pep asked.

'Just a couple of days. Thought I might do some fishing while I was here.'

'Fishing?' Pep was taken aback.

'Good for the head, so I'm told.'

'Not very good for the fish, though, eh?' Pep laughed and then grew serious. 'I can understand you wantin' to be alone with yourself at a time like this. Take a bit of getting over.'

'I've got a room all ready for you,' Emma chipped in.

'No, Emm. I've booked into an hotel in the town.'

'Why, no.' She was horrified at the thought. 'I wouldn't hear of it! you can—'

'You heard what he said,' Pep snapped, glaring at her, 'didn't you? He's staying in an hotel.'

An awkward silence fell, which Jed broke. 'It's best, Emm. I've got long-distance calls to make and what have you.'

Emma nodded meekly and Pep headed for the door. 'What time do you want your dinner tonight, Pep?' she asked.

'I don't know yet,' he said. 'I'll ring. See you later.'

'See you later,' Jed said with a nod.

'Have you told him yet?' Pep asked Emma as he went out. Emma shook her head.

'Told him what?' Jed asked as Pep disappeared and Beckie came in half draped in a bridesmaid's dress and humming, 'Here Comes The Bride'. 'What's this?' Jed asked the child. 'You getting married?'

'No,' Emma said quietly, 'but her mam is.' Silence fell again. 'Well, aren't you goin' to say congratulations, or something?'

Jed hugged her, partly so that she couldn't see the consternation in his face. 'Congratulations,' he said, flatly.

Jed's next stop was Archie's shed, down by the river, among the allotments. He could hear

30

the sound of a milling machine from outside and found Archie deep in concentration as he produced a cocktail shaker, lifting it out with tongs and dropping it, sizzling, into cold water. 'Mine's a double,' Jed said, 'shaken, not stirred.'

'Shite!' Archie jumped, losing his concentration, and the machine sliced the next shaker in half.

'Losing your touch there, kidder,' Jed said.

'That's thirty pee down the drain!' Archie protested.

'It'll make a good paperweight.' Jed came forward to shake his old friend by the hand.

'I thought you were in jail.'

'Don't believe what you read in the papers,' Jed said. 'Ninety per cent lies and ten per cent gossip.'

'Can't argue with pictures, though, can you?' Archie pointed to the press cutting stuck to the wall, which showed Jed being arrested. They wandered back out into the fresh air. Walter Fines, their old boss, was pulling vegetables out of the ground and waved at Jed.

'I thought you were locked up, lad,' he called out.

'Day release, for good behaviour.'

'Well, watch what you're doing, mind.'

'I'm kidding, Walter.'

'What?' Walter was confused and Jed waved at him to get on with his gardening.

'Nothing changes, does it?' he said to Archie.

'Oh,' Archie said, staring at Jed's Porsche, 'I don't know.'

'That's not mine,' Jed said quickly. 'They just lent us it.'

'Free?' Jed nodded and Archie scratched his head. 'Funny, isn't it? When you've got nowt you can't get nowt, and when you're loaded they're hoying it at you!' He looked at Jed curiously. 'What did you come back for?'

'Just to see everybody. If that's all right with you?'

'Fine by me, kid. Nice to see you.'

'How's things, then?'

'Up here?' Archie shook his head. 'Flat as a Jap's face.'

'Plenty of new cars on the roads.'

'Oh, aye. Debt's boomin'. Pep's testament to that. Things've changed, though. It's not the same. Everyone's out for what they can get. There's nae sense of . . .' He thought for a moment. 'Well, there's just nae bloody sense. We're having our weekly reunion tonight at the Legion. We get a discount on the beer since Bobby got made the club steward.'

'At the Legion?' Jed was amazed. 'Bobby was never in the army.'

'Said he was in the Falklands.' Archie shrugged. 'It was the only way he could get the job. Bought a bag of medals at a car boot sale and made up a load of stories.'

'Where there's a will . . .'

'. . . there's a wangle, eh?'

As they walked towards the car Jed pulled Wendy's business card from his pocket and looked at it. 'Have you got a fishing rod, Archie?' he asked.

'Pop Star Goes Fishin',' Archie laughed. 'There's one for the *Evening Chronicle*. Where you plannin' on gannin'?'

'Tynemouth,' Jed said.

The British Legion Club was above a shop in the city centre's Big Market. No one would have found it if they didn't know where to look. Jed thought he was going to burst out laughing when he saw Bobby taking some drinks across to some old boys, his blazer festooned with medal ribbons.

'No singing, mind,' Bobby warned when he saw Jed sitting with Walter, Omo, Big Chrissie and Young Paul. 'Against the rules.'

'Right you are, Sarge.' Jed gave a mock salute.

'Rock star!' Omo laughed. 'I thought you were locked up.'

'Y'ever see that movie where Steve McQueen jumped over the fence on the motorbike?'

'*The Great Escape?*' Big Chrissie asked.

'That's me,' Jed nodded.

'It's never off the telly,' Omo said.

'I held three prison officers hostage, then I got a helicopter to come in low, over the roof, and then up, up and away.'

'He never got over the fence, did he?' Walter mused, almost to himself.

'Who?' Archie wanted to know.

'Steve McQueen. He got tangled up in all the barbed wire. And then, er . . .' Walter racked his memory. 'Then they took him back to the prison camp.'

'So, how did you get out?' Paul wanted to know.

'I was never in, man!' Jed was beginning to get irritated by the constant references to jail. 'I have *not* been to prison!'

'Fifth Dimension!' Omo interjected.

'What about it?' Big Chrissie wanted to know.

'"Up, Up and Away", that's who sung it. The Fifth Dimension.' To prove his point he started to croon the song.

'Bloody dementia,' Archie groaned, just as Tony arrived, dressed from head to foot in the latest cycling gear, covered in grease and oil.

'Oh, howway, now Tony,' Bobby said, frowning at the new arrival. 'You know the dress code, son. I can't let you in like that.'

'I came straight from work. To see Jed.' Tony winked. 'I promise I'll not mention the Falklands.' Bobby sank into a silent fury at this blatant blackmail. 'When did they let you out?' Tony asked Jed.

'They didn't!' Jed wailed despairingly.

'He escaped,' Big Chrissie informed him.

'In a helicopter,' Omo added.

'Nah.' Tony was impressed, ''Sright?'

'But Steve McQueen got all tangled up in barbed wire,' Paul said.

'Steve McQueen?' Tony looked puzzled. 'I thought he was dead.'

'Dear God Almighty!' Jed took a long drink and started to laugh. He had missed this sort of thing a lot down south.

As the evening wore on the group continued to talk and drink. Eventually the doors were locked and only they remained, as Big Chrissie explained to the others the little business venture he and Omo were setting up.

'We buy a job lot, right, from the Indian lads in Manchester. Seconds, like. You get thirteen dozen pairs of knickers, in a box, for a hundred quid. Then, we mix a, like, potion kind of thing, in a vat. Pour this special stuff in, what Omo's mate's concocted for us . . .'

'Cyril,' Omo chipped in. 'He used to be a chemist. Now he's on the Nat King.'

'And then we hoy all the knickers in . . .'

'Gi' them a good stir round . . .'

'. . . an' then empty them out. They come out smelling of . . .' Big Chrissie thought for a moment. 'The way they would be smelling, had they been worn, see?'

Jed nodded. 'We're talking soiled panties here, are we?'

'Right.' Big Chrissie smiled happily. 'And then Omo takes them out into the back garden and rubs the gusset on the grass, and that's it.'

'How does that make you money?' Walter asked, completely bamboozled.

''Cause dirty old buggers like you's willing to pay good money for them,' Omo explained.

'Not me!' Walter protested.

'How much?' Archie wanted to know.

'A fiver a time. We put a little note in, an' all.' Chrissie attempted a young girl's voice: 'Dear Sir, I hope you enjoy my knickers . . .'

'Nah,' said Archie. Even he was having trouble swallowing this.

'We're all set to go,' Omo assured him. 'We've had orders from as far away as Gibraltar.'

'Thirteen dozen pairs,' said Big Chrissie. 'How many's that?'

Omo struggled with the mental arithmetic for a moment and then gave up. 'Loads!'

'Who writes the notes?' Archie asked.

'Omo. His handwriting looks more like a lassie's.'

'At least I can bloody write!' Omo blustered, as the others sat in silence trying to take in what they'd just been told. 'We're bringing out a catalogue shortly.'

'Of what?' Jed wanted to know.

'Sex aid . . . things,' Big Chrissie said.

'You know it's illegal to send that stuff through the post, don't you?' Jed asked.

'Really?' Omo feigned horror.

Archie, taking a slurp from his drink, decided to change the subject. 'So,' he said to Jed, 'do you miss us? Where you are, then?'

'I think about you lot a lot, believe it or not.'

'Aye,' Bobby said, 'guilt. But do you miss us?'

'I think about you.'

'Reduced to a distant memory,' Archie opined. 'How sad.'

'How can you live like that,' Bobby asked, 'amongst all them people?'

'What people?' Jed knew what he meant but wasn't about to give him the satisfaction of letting on.

36

'Them posh twats in the country. It's worse than London for sleaze, you know. Wife-swappin', an' all that.'

'You'd know, would you?' Tony asked.

'I've been to them places for picnics!'

'Sounds all right to me,' Omo said, 'wife-swapping.'

'Who's gonna take your lass?' Big Chrissie asked. 'The blind man?'

'That's offensive,' Omo protested.

'So is she!'

'It's not like that, man,' Jed said, interrupting their banter. 'It's all right. Plus I get left alone. Nobody bothers me down there. Yet.'

'Sunnier down there an' all, I'll bet,' Archie said. 'Y're that bit nearer the Equator, y'see.'

'You're nearer all the ferry ports an' all,' Bobby pointed out. 'All them bloody immigrants flooding in from abroad. Telling lies just to further their own ends.'

'That's how you got the job here!' Archie pointed out.

'Shh,' hissed Bobby looking panicked, 'for Christ's sake.'

'Is this how people get by?' Jed asked Archie.

'It is up here, kid.'

Jed felt a sudden attack of guilt. 'Well, there's an open invitation to you all to come and stay, you know.'

'Everybody?'

'Why aye. You can all kip at my gaff. There's plenty of room. I've got ten toilets, you know.'

There was a moment's silence before they all

broke into cheers, patting Jed on the back and happily accepting his invitation.

'I always said he'd never forget his mates,' Big Chrissie said.

'I always said he'd never forget his home town,' Bobby agreed.

'Eeh, what a lying bunch of bastards,' Omo said.

'Pina Coladas all round then, is it?' Jed enquired.

'In here?' Omo laughed. 'Yee'll be lucky.'

As Jed went to replenish the drinks he felt good, but wondered just what he might have let himself in for.

One of the main reasons he had come back North was in the hope of finding Wendy. The only clues he had were her card, which had only a box number, and the fact that she had told him she lived in Tynemouth, overlooking the water. The following day he took Archie's fishing gear and settled himself down against the sea wall, letting the rod dangle in the water as he pondered all the things that had been happening. On the way to and from the car he tried to peer into people's front rooms, without drawing attention to himself, in the hope that he might suddenly see her. The only people he came into contact with were a bunch of young girls with autograph books. In a house overlooking the sea wall one of his songs was playing. He listened for a few seconds, then walked dejectedly back to the Porsche.

Emma opened the door to him herself this time.

'Hiya,' he said, making an effort to sound bright and breezy. 'I just popped by to say ta-ra, pet. I'm gonna head off back to—' He broke off and lifted her face up to the light. Her eye was swollen and puffy. 'Cold sore, eh?'

'Jed, look—'

'I am looking, Emma, and I don't like what I see. Where's Pep?'

She shook her head. She obviously had no intention of telling him. Jed turned quickly and strode back to his car. 'Oh, please, Jed. Don't go over there causing trouble. It's not what you think.'

Without looking back he drove straight to the converted Victorian buildings that housed Pep's office. Pep's car was just drawing up as he got there.

'Hey, Pep!' Jed called out.

'What?' Pep, carrying a briefcase, was obviously in a hurry.

'That bruise, under Emma's eye.'

'What bruise?'

'You're not raising your hands to her, are you?'

'Why no, man. Divvent be so daft.'

'So, how did she get the shiner, then?'

'Search me, bonny lad.'

'If I find out otherwise, Pep, I'll do more than search you.'

'Hey,' Pep shouted angrily, 'what gives you the right to go poking your bugle into other people's affairs?'

'She's my sister, Pep.'

'And she's my wife, Jed.'

'Not yet she's not.'

'As good as.'

'Well, then, treat her the way you're supposed to treat a wife.' Jed was getting dangerously close to hitting Pep. 'Do you understand?'

'I understand, Jed, but you don't.' Pep gave a whistle and two burly guys came out of the offices, heading towards them. Pep raised his hand and they stopped, like two well-trained dogs. 'You see, Jed, things've changed a bit since you've been away on your travels. I no longer deal in twopenny ha'penny credit. Nowadays I deal in other things.'

'What kind of things?'

'All kinds of things, and I don't have to put up with any lip any longer, neither.'

Jed laughed. 'You wouldn't be threatening me, Pep, would you?'

Pep laughed too. 'What? When we're ganna be brothers-in-law?' He went to put his arm round Jed but Jed pushed him away. 'Accusing someone of something when you don't have any evidence can be dangerous, Jed. You of all people should know that.'

'I meant what I said, Pep. If I find out you've been knocking Emma about I'll take it out of your face.' He opened his car door. 'And don't be thinking Tick and Tock over there are gonna save you.' With that passing shot he drove off, leaving Pep fuming.

The elderly porter manning the reception desk at Jed's hotel seemed to be living life at a third of normal speed. He eventually managed to add up the bill and took Jed's credit card. 'There's a message for you somewhere,' he said, rummaging under a pile of paper. 'Here we are – from a Miss . . . er, Lucy, who is' – he squinted at the note – 'Adrian's sister. Can she see you urgently in London?'

'Can I see that?' As Jed took the message the credit card machine beeped. This, Jed knew, was a warning, telling the porter that the company was declining the transaction and instructing him to retain the card.

'Oh,' the old man said, looking flustered, 'Dear me.'

'Never mind,' Jed said quickly. 'I'll pay cash.' He pulled out his fast-diminishing bundle of readies and settled the bill, before setting off for London at speed.

CHAPTER FOUR

Jed pulled up in front of the Carlton Hotel, climbed out of the car, stretched his aching limbs and went in. A late-model Jaguar was parked across the square with the lights off. Three silhouettes inside were watching the hotel entrance.

Lucy was waiting in the shiny marbled foyer on a settee. At her feet was a cardboard box with papers visible inside.

'Hello,' Jed said as she got up to greet him. 'I got your message. The guy said it was urgent.'

'Did he?' she seemed surprised.

'Isn't it?'

She shook her head. 'Not really. I just . . . I've got that stuff I told you about, and I wanted to give it to you. Wanted it out of the house.' They took the box up to Jed's suite. 'It's just some stuff that got dumped at my place,' she explained once they were sitting down. 'I thought you should see it, in case it's of any importance to you.'

'Thanks. I'll go through it, see if there's anything I should know about. What would you like me to do with it?'

She shrugged. 'Whatever. Give it to the police, I suppose. It'll no doubt disappear into a bureaucratic black hole somewhere. How was the old home town?'

'Looked the same, as I stepped down from the train, and there to meet me, was—'

'Your girlfriend?' She interrupted his Tom Jones impression.

'Nope,' he said, and grinned. 'Situation vacant there. How about you?'

She shook her head and Jed felt more pleased than he would have expected. 'Have you heard anything more from the police?' she asked.

'Not yet. I'll speak to them again in the morning. Then I'll have to head off down to Wiltshire. Try and get this bloody album finished.'

'I really appreciate your concern over Adrian, Jed. There weren't many people who cared.' As they looked at each other there was a buzz of desire in the air. He wanted to take things further, and suspected that she did, too, but both seemed to sense that the timing was wrong. A suspicious thought suddenly edged into Jed's mind.

'If you're Adrian's only surviving relative, all his royalties and earnings and stuff will come to you, won't they?'

'I suppose so.' She seemed startled by the thought. 'It never crossed my mind.' Jed wondered if he was being naïve and she saw the doubt in his eyes. 'I'll have to go, Jed.'

'Is there anything more I can do?'

'You've done it already. You gave Adrian success. It was all he'd ever wanted in his entire life.' She kissed him on the mouth before turning and leaving him confused. The kiss seemed to be for real, but how could he tell? She was Adrian's sister, after all, and everyone knew how devious *he* could be.

Jed rummaged around inside the box, bringing out files, receipts, tapes, lyrics and a tatty old telephone answering machine.

Outside, in the Jaguar, the three men saw Lucy leaving the hotel. One of them was Connors. 'She ain't got the box no more,' said one of his companions.

'Must've left it upstairs,' Connors muttered.

'Why couldn't we just take it off her in the street?'

'I refuse to answer that question,' Connors snapped, 'on the grounds that it's too dumb.'

The answering machine had no plug on it so Jed ejected the cassette, slipped it into his beat-box and switched it on.

'. . . Mr Lynn,' said a metallic voice, 'this is Kellie from Kurtz car rental. I'm chasing up a bill for a Jaguar XJS over the May bank holiday weekend. There seems to have been a problem with your credit card.'

'You as well?' Jed laughed.

'. . . Hello Ade.' An angry woman's voice filled the room. 'This is Sue. Regarding our date. Thanks for standing me up, you arsehole. Don't bother ringing me again.' She paused. 'Well, leave it a week, eh? Bye . . .'

'What a lad.' Jed shook his head in reluctant admiration.

'. . . Mr Lynn, this is Tony from Travel Corp. We have you booked on the Concorde for New York this Thursday. Could you give me a call please, regarding the bill? Thanks a lot. Bye . . .'

'. . . Adrian.' A new, more nervous voice. Male again. 'What the hell's going on? You promised me the transfer would go through today and nothing's turned up. Made me look a right fool, you have. I don't think you realise how serious this is. They're not happy at this end. The boss is going apeshit. Threatening all kinds of things. You know what'll happen if you default once more, don't you? This isn't a game, Ade!'

'. . . Hi, Adrian.' A familiar voice. 'This is Roxanne down in the country. Please could you ring me as soon as you can. Jed threatened to kill you this morning. *Auf wiedersehen.*'

'Great!' Jed felt that things were getting worse, not better. The best thing, he decided, was to take the tape straight to the police.

McClusky listened to the frightened male voice with Jed, and then switched the machine off. 'Do you have any idea who that is?' he asked.

Jed shook his head. 'Do you think it could be . . . you know . . . whoever . . .?'

'It could be anyone, Mr Shepperd. You said yourself Mr Lynn had a lot of enemies.'

'Yes, but that's a threat.'

McClusky shrugged. 'Leave it with me. I'll look into it. Is there anything else on there?'

'Nothing of importance.' McClusky raised an eyebrow and switched the tape back on again, listening to Roxanne's message. He then looked at Jed, who swallowed hard. 'Ah, that. That was just a joke!'

Back at the Carlton Jed made his way to the reception. 'I'm leaving first thing,' he told the clerk. 'Can I have my bill made up, please?'

'Of course, sir.' The clerk looked over to the duty manager, who made his way across.

'Mr Shepperd.' The manager was as smooth as silk. 'We rang your credit card number for authorisation, and I'm afraid—'

'Don't tell me. It was declined.'

'I'm afraid so.'

'What's the damage?' Jed pulled out what was left of his cash float.

The suite was in darkness when he reached it. He pressed the lights but nothing happened. He heard a noise but before he could react three bodies leapt on him, bringing him down to the floor, landing painful kicks and punches. Almost drifting into unconsciousness he saw an angry, menacing face stooping over him. Mustering his strength he punched hard between his legs and the face contorted into a scream as the man reeled back. Jed rolled to one side, pulled himself to his feet and ran out of the room.

'Kill the bastard!' The voice could only have been that of his assailant – the half shouted, half gasped command of one who has been punched in the balls.

Jed dashed for the fire escape. Out in the fresh

air he felt better and hurtled down the metal steps, hearing the two men clattering behind him. They were gaining ground as he jumped over the balcony and landed in a large pile of rubbish bags, which burst under the impact. He jumped back onto his feet and ran to the end of the alley as the men climbed over the edge of the fire escape to follow him. Jed flagged down a passing taxi, threw himself into the back. 'Liverpool Street Station, please,' he panted as the taxi pulled away with the two men running along behind. Within a few yards the cab had gained enough speed and the men were left gasping for air in the road.

Bowles showed no emotion in his face as Connors, still pale from his painful ordeal, tried to explain how they had failed. 'We tore the place apart, but we couldn't find anything. It would've helped if we'd known what we were supposed to be looking for.'

'This.' Detective Inspector McClusky, who was sitting with Bowles in his apartment, held up the cassette from the answering machine.

'What is it?' Connors asked.

McClusky said nothing, inserting the tape in Bowles' hi-fi and pressing the button. Connors' voice crackled through the expensive speakers. '. . . the boss is going apeshit, threatening all kinds of things . . .'

'Where the hell did that come from?' Connors looked aghast.

'Jed Shepperd gave it to me. Tonight,' McClusky informed him.

'Can we destroy it?'

'We could,' McClusky said, 'but if I was him I'd have made a copy. Wouldn't you?' Connors looked across to Bowles for help, but Bowles remained impassive. 'So Jed Shepperd knows what's on the tape. He doesn't know who the voice is yet. But that's only a matter of time.'

Both McClusky and Connors fell silent, waiting for Bowles to speak. He pondered for a moment. 'We need to discredit Shepperd,' he said eventually, 'disgrace him. Convince people he's responsible for Adrian Lynn's death. It's essential that no one believes a word he says.'

'How can we do that?' Connors asked.

'We have him locked up.' Bowles looked at McClusky. 'I want you to sort it so's some of your mob pay Mr Shepperd a visit.' He turned to Connors. 'And I want you to make sure there's something worth finding when they turn up.' They both looked doubtful, for different reasons. 'We don't have a choice. It's him or us. By the way' – he turned to McClusky – 'was there anything else on the cassette?'

McClusky nodded, surprised at Bowles's guess, and switched Roxanne's message on. Bowles smiled when he heard it. *Better than I'd dared hope*, he thought. 'That's my girl,' he murmured.

Jed made it back to the security of Studley House and to Roxanne, who appeared to be nervous, although Jed was too preoccupied with his own thoughts to ask her why. 'I spoke with the banks, Jed,' she told him. 'All the withdrawals were

49

legitimate. It seems that you have a major funding problem.'

'That can't be right, man. All the money I had, or thought I had, is suddenly not there?'

'It looks like that is the situation.'

'But I haven't withdrawn anything. What's gonna happen here, to all this?' He gestured around him. 'To the Jag, and the Jeep, and me Triumph? They're all on a direct debit! My mates'll be arriving from Newcastle shortly. How can I look after them if I'm potless?'

'Can't you get another advance out of your record company?'

'Good thinking, Roxanne. They said they were behind me all the way. And after you've done that, ring Paddington Green Police Station. There's a man called McClusky I need to talk to.'

Jed left her to make the calls and went through to the studio, picking up his Telecaster and pulling on some headphones, which were connected to the mixing desk. He sat, strumming the guitar for several moments, trying to lose himself in his work. Then suddenly his headphones were silent. He was aware only of the empty, impotent ring of unamplified strings, suddenly robbed of their power to thrill.

He turned quickly to see that two men had come into the room behind him – one still holding the plug he had wrenched from the power socket.

'Hoy!' Jed jumped. 'What the hell are you doing?' The man held up a piece of paper. 'What's that?'

'A search warrant.'

The first man came in from the other room holding up a polythene bag full of white powder. 'Well,' he said, 'look what we've got here.'

'What?' Jed was mystified.

Just as the police were leading Jed out to a waiting police car, two cabs pulled into the drive, disgorging an astonished bunch of Geordie men. They stood, stunned, watching their mate, and host, being put into the back of the patrol car.

'There's cold beer in the fridge, lads,' Jed called out, before being driven away.

CHAPTER FIVE

'The charge is one of possession,' the clerk read out to the court, 'of a controlled drug, namely cocaine, with intent to supply, contrary to Section Five, Subsection Three, of the Misuse of Drugs Act of 1971.' Jed was in the dock, flanked by two security officers. He was unshaven and wearing the same clothes he had been arrested in. Roxanne sat behind him, looking glum. 'Particulars are that on the day of November the seventh, 1996, Gerald Shepperd had in his possession two hundred and twenty grams of a controlled drug of Class A, namely cocaine.'

'I'm not guilty,' Jed shouted angrily and a ripple of excitement passed through the jackals of the media who packed the press gallery. 'I'm no bloody drug dealer! Hasn't anybody been listening to what I've been saying here? I'm not guilty. D'you hear?'

'You're not required to enter a plea at this stage, Mr Shepperd,' the magistrate informed him. 'This is simply a bail hearing. Do you understand?' Jed nodded silently, too angry to trust himself to speak civilly.

'Mr Shepperd,' the clerk continued, 'are you legally represented here today?'

'I've not had a chance to organise any of that yet.'

'It's the law of the land that you have a right to proper legal representation, and that if you cannot afford such, then the court is obliged, via legal aid, to appoint such. Can you afford such?' The clerk looked towards Roxanne, who shook her head.

'Really?' The magistrate was obviously taken aback by this revelation and shook his head in despair at the financial incompetence of the pop world. 'Very well. Application for legal aid is noted. In view of the gravity of the charges, not to mention the quantities of drugs involved, bail will be granted if a surety is willing to guarantee a sum of one hundred thousand pounds.'

'A hundred grand?' Jed was staggered. 'I can't afford that!'

'I would warn you, Mr Shepperd,' the magistrate continued, 'that, should you be found guilty, the court can order the confiscation of the profits of lucrative drug trafficking when sentencing the offender.' He turned to the clerk. 'The defendant will be remanded in custody until further hearing.'

As Jed was led from the dock in a state of shock, the press stampeded from the gallery, heading for the phones. One of the fastest was Ted Quimby, a man who looked more like a successful young solicitor than a gutter reporter. He dictated down the phone, '. . . it's all gone wrong for Geordie Jed . . .'

The only phone not being used by a reporter

was in the hands of Connors. 'It's all going according to plan,' he said. 'Couldn't have got a better result if we'd owned the magistrate. I don't think Shepperd'll be seeing the light of day for a long, long time.'

'Oh,' Bowles' voice purred from the other end of the line, 'how sad. Bye bye, country boy.'

Roxanne was allowed to visit Jed in one of the holding cells. 'What about an advance from the record company?' Jed asked her. 'They said they'd help.'

She shook her head. 'They have already paid for an album. They also paid Adrian advances against future royalties, on albums after this one. I don't think they'll pay anything more until they get something back.'

'They never paid *me* anything!' Jed protested. 'I've not seen a penny of it.'

'But they paid Adrian, via First Ade Management. Legally it's just the same.'

'Let me get this straight. The record company, via First Ade Management, have already paid me three hundred thousand pounds for my next album?'

'Right.'

'Plus about a hundred thousand more than they were ever obliged to?'

'Right.'

'But there's no money left in any of my bank accounts to pay for anything? And even if there was, I couldn't fulfil my contractual obligations because I'm in jail. And I can't get out, 'cause I can't afford the bail. That it?'

'That's it.'

Jed considered his predicament for a moment. 'So, I'm up shit creek in a barbed-wire canoe?' Roxanne, although slightly confused by the vocabulary, got his drift and nodded reluctantly. 'I don't know what's going on here, Roxanne,' he sighed, 'but I do know that it's rotten. And if I'm gonna clear my name, I've got to get out of here. How am I gonna do that?'

'Dynamite?'

'That's not funny, Roxanne.'

'I'm sorry. I don't know what else to suggest.'

Emma was equally at a loss as to how to help her brother as she lay in bed beside her husband-to-be, staring at the wall. The only person she could think of turning to was Pep, and she knew that he and Jed did not exactly hold each other in high regard.

'It's not just that it would all but empty the bank account, pet.' Pep was pleading his case from the other side of the bed. 'If I put this bail money up, and anything were to happen, I'd have to mortgage the entire business.'

Emma remained silent, letting him come round to the idea in his own time. 'But' – he propped himself up on one elbow and peeped over her shoulder – 'if your big brother means that much to you . . .'

Emma's eyes lit up and she turned over to face him, so happy that he was actually willing to do this for her.

'Mind,' Pep muttered as she all but smothered

him with affection, 'where the hell all his own money's gone I don't know.'

Jed was asleep on his bunk when the policeman threw open the door and shouted, 'Shepperd!'

He sat up with a start. 'Yeah?'

'Your bail's been met. You're free to go, subject to the bail conditions.'

Jed climbed off the bunk. 'A hundred grand?'

'To the last ha'penny. Must be nice to have friends with that sort of money.'

'Does it say which friend stumped it up?'

The policeman studied a bunch of faxes in his hand. 'A Mr . . . Albert Peploe of Newcastle.'

'Pep!' Jed was flabbergasted. Perhaps he had had Pep wrong all this time.

'Conditions of bail are that you're not allowed to leave the country, your passport is to be retained by the court, and you've to report to your local police station every day. Do you have your passport with you?'

Jed laughed. 'Aye, it's hidden down me sock.'

The policeman's face showed no glimmer of amusement. 'Then please make the necessary arrangements to have it delivered here forthwith.'

Jed felt a shudder of relief run down his spine as he walked out behind the uniformed man. That, he thought to himself, was too close for comfort.

When he got back to Studley and went out to the pool, the guys gave him a rousing cheer. Empties were strewn all around them and Joe the gardener was trying to tidy up while still keeping his distance.

'Yes,' Omo shouted, 'here he is, the convict!'

'You look like shite, son,' Archie told him.

'I've had better days, Archie. Any of those beers left?'

Omo handed him a bottle. 'Get that one down your neck. I'll get some more.'

'We got a bit of stuff in,' Archie explained as Jed took a deep swig. 'You were running low on certain essential items.'

'Like cocaine an' all that,' Omo shouted over his shoulder.

'Very funny,' Jed shouted back and then settled down with Archie. 'Eeh well, I didn't expect all this when I invited you lot down here. I'm sitting here without the price of a pint in my pocket. It's embarrassing.'

'Divvent worry about it, Jed,' Archie reassured him.

'Don't worry? My manager's been topped, the finger's being pointed at me and I'm on bail for dealing drugs.'

Archie nodded. 'I take it back.'

'What are you gonna do?' Big Chrissie asked.

'I don't know. I haven't had a chance to think.'

'Cushy gaff, mind, Jed,' Omo said, returning with three more six-packs. 'Ten toilets! If me bowels was more regular, I'd be spoilt for choice!'

'I'm glad you like it,' Jed said. 'You'd better make the most of it.'

'Hello, son.' Walter woke up with a jerk. 'You broken out of jail again?'

As the evening came down and the underwater lights of the pool began to show, Jed went to his studio, hoping to get some work done and take his mind off his troubles. Once he was ready, he turned up the volume, and let the time slip by.

It was two hours later when Omo popped his head round the door, shouting to be heard. 'Want a cup of tea?' he bellowed. 'I said—'

'Yeah, all right. I'm gonna knock this on the head in a minute.'

'Sounding cushy,' Omo said and disappeared off to the kitchen as Jed started to switch off for the night. Once everything was unplugged he followed Omo down the corridor and noticed that Roxanne's bedroom door was open. Looking in, he discovered her sorting through her personal belongings, apparently putting things in order. He knew what that meant.

'When?' he asked, leaning against the door frame.

'Soon,' Roxanne said, sadly. 'I have to make a living, Jed, and you can't afford to pay me right now. I know it's not your fault, but—'

'You don't want to wait until I get all this sorted out? I'm gonna be talking to the lawyers in the morning, and then—'

'Jed,' she said slowly, her face more serious now than Jed had ever seen it, 'this is going to take more than a talk with your lawyers to sort out. It's heavy, and . . . well . . .' She seemed to be searching for the right words. 'I want to be able to work in this business again.'

Jed nodded his head. He could see the sense in

what she was saying. 'You've done a wonderful job here, Roxanne. I thank you for that. I know Adrian would've wanted to thank you too.' He dropped his head, feeling too choked up to say any more, and Roxanne's eyes filled with tears.

'Hey,' she said, her voice cracking, 'we had some fun, didn't we?'

'We certainly did.' He forced himself to sound cheerful. They stared at each other for a second. 'You don't think I killed Adrian, do you?'

'I *know* you didn't!' The emphasis she put on the words surprised him, but he put it down to her accent.

'So, this is goodbye, then?'

'I guess so.' They were both thinking the same thing, but it didn't look as if Jed was going to pluck up the courage to say anything. 'Would you like to come in and close the door?' she asked.

The door closed just as Omo arrived outside with a couple of mugs of tea. He put his ear to the panels and then looked down at the tea. 'You'll not be wanting this, I take it,' he said quietly to himself.

The following morning Alan Clarke was in his office at Paradigm Records with his boss, Dick Pilsbury, a tall, oily man. On the wall, behind Clarke's head, hung a multi-platinum plaque, awarded to him for Jed's *Crocodile Shoes* album sales. Both men were listening to Clarke's secretary as she read back a letter Pilsbury had just dictated.

'. . . and in the absence of an album by the

agreed aforementioned date, herewith we formally request the return of all moneys paid to First Ade Management representing advances. These advances were paid in good faith against the delivery of your next album. Paradigm's position is that no further advances will be made to you. Yours truly . . .'

'Fax it to Shepperd,' Pilsbury instructed her, 'and copy the lawyers.'

'Yes, Mr Pilsbury.' She rose and left the room.

Clarke shook his head. He felt deeply unhappy. 'Do we really want to do this, Dick? I mean, all this publicity! It's priceless. And it's free! Everyone's gonna want Jed Shepperd's next album, good or bad. The press coverage alone — you couldn't buy this kind of thing. It's bordering on the O.J. Simpson.'

'And you reckon that's all right, do you?' Pilsbury asked, obviously unimpressed by Clarke's arguments. 'Morally?'

'Morally?' Clarke couldn't believe what he was hearing. 'When Jed was ringing here asking for your help, you were the one insisting that no one take his calls.' He pointed to the platinum discs on the wall. 'Look, Dick, the only people who can put you up on that wall are the punters, and they want another Jed Shepperd record.'

'I wanted another Jed Shepperd record,' Pilsbury was suddenly shouting, 'to the point where I laid out almost half a million pounds, which by all accounts he's stuffed up his nose!' He took a deep breath and regained some of his composure.

'The punters will get over it. They're blessed with short memories, thank God.'

'You could at least give the guy some downtime. We have studios standing idle and salaried engineers doing nothing.'

Pilsbury mustered all his senior management training and smiled understandingly. 'Alan, it's understandable you're upset. He was your signing. But the board feel that Paradigm, as a publicly quoted company, cannot afford to be perceived to be positively endorsing such people.'

'"Such people" are the lifeblood of this business, I'd remind you,' Clarke snapped. 'No them, no us.'

'Orders is orders.' Pilsbury shrugged. 'Get over it.'

'This is disgusting, even by *our* standards.'

Pilsbury chose that moment to leave Clarke, still fuming with frustration and rage. Following orders was not one of the things Clarke had joined the music industry to do. In his anger he snapped his favourite pencil in half.

Pilsbury went back to his office, glanced briefly at the man sitting there, expectantly, and poured himself a tumbler of whisky. 'Done,' he said curtly.

'Good.' Bowles took a sip from an identical tumbler.

'It wasn't easy. Alan Clarke's a tenacious little bastard.'

'Tenacious, but not suspicious?' Pilsbury shook his head and Bowles raised his glass with a satisfied smile. 'Here's to Cut-Outs, then.' Pilsbury glanced at the door nervously, hoping nobody could overhear Bowles. 'Long may they continue, eh?' They both drank a toast to one of the most notorious and illegal of music-business practices. 'I hear you've been looking to buy abroad, Dick. Big house with a pool and tennis court, right?' Pilsbury gave a smug little nod and Bowles' expression grew instantly cold. 'If I can hear about it, then so could others. You hearing me?' Bowles put his drink down and left Pilsbury to consider his own carelessness.

The arrival of the fax at Studley House seemed to knock the final bit of stuffing out of Jed. Roxanne watched as he read, studying his face for reaction. Omo and Archie came in as he finished reading it.

'Roxanne!' Omo burst out laughing. 'Rock star knobbin' last night, was he? Pork sword a go-go?' He clenched his fists and thrust his loins back and forth in a lewd pantomime of sex. Archie elbowed him in the ribs to shut him up. 'What?'

'I take it that's not from the lottery people,' Archie said, pointing at the fax.

'It's from my record company. They either want an album, or their money back.'

'We could have a whipround,' Omo suggested.

'Four hundred grand?' Jed said. 'That's an awful lot of whipping.'

'Me and the lads have been talking, Jed,' Archie said, 'and we reckon it's time we all went home.'

'What?' Jed had been lost in his own thoughts. 'Oh, right. I don't blame you. I'd like to be coming along.'

'When I said "we", Jed, I meant "we".'

Jed looked at him for a moment, his mind racing. 'I can't come, man. I've got to report to the local cop shop every day.'

'Well you can't stay here and just wait for the porridge,' Archie protested. 'That's micey if you're innocent!'

'If you went back on the road, and then got nicked,' Omo suggested, 'they'd bang you up in Durham, which would be easier for visiting.'

'You won't forget your appointment, Jed,' Roxanne interrupted.

'Oh, yeah!' Jed came back to reality. 'I'm off to see the legal eagles.'

'Shite-hawks more like,' Archie laughed bitterly.

CHAPTER SIX

Wendy had thought about Jed a great deal since their chance meeting, and had closely followed his misfortunes in the media. She looked at the situation from every possible angle and decided that she simply couldn't give up that easily. There had to be a way of making contact with him again. She started with a phone call to Paradigm and was put through to Alan Clarke's secretary. 'Alan has left, and I'm afraid Jed Shepperd is not with Paradigm Records any more,' she was told. 'I suggest you try the police or his fan club.'

Neither of these options, she felt, was likely to produce the desired result. She had to find some more personal way of getting in touch. Wandering around her front room, racking her brains, she picked up a copy of the local newspaper and her eye was drawn to a picture of Emma on the front page and the headline, OUR JED IS INNOCENT, SAYS POP STAR'S SISTER. Wendy skimmed through the article until she found what she was looking for: '". . . couldn't be guilty of such a thing," said Ms Shepperd, of Castle Farm Villas, South Gosforth.' It might not be a full address, but it was close enough to bring a triumphant smile to Wendy's lips.

*   *   *

Lucy was pursuing her goals with equal tenacity, sitting patiently in front of the desk sergeant at Paddington Green Police Station, waiting for Detective Inspector McClusky.

'I can't guarantee he'll show up, miss,' the sergeant said.

'That's all right.' Lucy was preparing herself for a long siege if necessary. She lost track of time after a while and then her moment arrived. The sergeant was in his inner office when she caught sight of someone else moving behind the scenes. Leaping from her chair she ran to the desk shouting, 'Inspector McClusky!' Her voice died away and silence fell over the room. She waited a few seconds but no one came out, so she started to shout again, setting up a chant: 'Inspector McClusky! Inspector McClusky! Inspector McClusky! Inspector McClusky!'

It worked and the inspector appeared at the desk. 'Miss Lynn. How nice to see you. Would you like to come through?' He led her through to his office and settled her down, getting them both cups of coffee.

'My brother dies, in suspicious circumstances' – Lucy spelt out her worries – 'and then, nothing. I end up having to chase the officer in charge of the investigation to find out if there've been any developments. Is this how it's meant to be?'

'I'm sorry, Miss Lynn. I've not been around much. But I'm here now. So, what exactly do you want to know?'

'What's happening?'

'We're proceeding with our investigations and,

when complete, a report will be sent to the coroner.'

'You are still treating my brother's death as suspicious?'

'We're treating Mr Lynn's death as *possibly* suspicious. It's a possibility. Along with various other possibilities.'

Lucy was becoming very angry. 'Do you think you could be a little more vague?'

'Miss Lynn, I understand your frustration. As soon as I've anything to tell you I'll be in touch.'

'I don't believe you. How many officers do you have working on this?'

'There are a number of officers working on—'

'How many?' she shouted.

'Miss Lynn,' he shouted back, 'the fact is that there are dozens of deaths each day—'

Lucy shot to her feet, apparently losing control. 'I don't care! I don't care about the others! I care about my brother!'

A uniformed officer came into the room to see what was happening but McClusky waved him out. He needed to deal with Lucy himself. 'We've interviewed literally dozens of people over the last few weeks. People who might've had reason to want your brother dead. But, up to now, the number-one contender, the prime suspect if you like, is Jed Shepperd.' Lucy shook her head wearily. 'And him being arrested and charged with drug-dealing makes me even more inclined to believe that—'

'Jed didn't kill Adrian,' she interrupted. 'I'm certain of it.'

'How can you be?' McClusky asked quietly, and Lucy felt her confusion grow even deeper. By the time she got back to her car she couldn't hold back the tears any more.

Before leaving Studley House, Roxanne tried to get Jed as straight as possible with his paperwork, spreading it out on the billiard table while Archie and Omo shot balls between the piles.

'These are copies of your financial accounts going back over the last couple of years,' she said. She could see that Jed was completely at a loss as he stared at the heaps of paper. 'I've had a look at them. I'm not an expert, but they seem to be in an awful muddle. There'll be plenty of time to sift through it all. The time between arrest and going to trial can be anything up to eighteen months, apparently. Did you ever bother to keep an eye on any of this?'

Jed shook his head mournfully. 'I left it all to my manager.'

'A lot of people tend to do that. It's usually a big mistake.'

Omo watched as Roxanne left the room. 'Can I just say . . . I'd love to shag her?' he said once she was safely out of earshot.

'So it could well be a spell in the jail?' Archie asked Jed.

'That's what the solicitor reckoned. He thinks they'll want to make an example of me.'

'Dear oh dear.'

'We've got a shed at the cemetery,' Omo said cheerfully, 'where we keep the coffins just before we plant them. You could hole up there.'

'I think I'd prefer the nick.'

'Have you still got your passport?' Archie asked.

'Yeah, but I've got to hand it in to the court.'

Archie raised an eyebrow. 'But you haven't handed it in yet?' Jed shook his head. 'Down to Dover, on the bike, with the skid-lid on so's nobody would recognise you . . .'

Omo took over: '. . . through the tunnel, late night, on the ghost train, nobody about . . .'

'. . . down through France, on into Spain . . .' Archie again.

'What's he ganna dae when he gets there?' Omo asked.

'He can sing for his supper. Plenty of that on the Continent, strumming in pubs an' the like.'

'Bit of a comedown after Wembley Arena,' Jed protested.

'Better than eating prison food,' Archie suggested.

'I can't do that.' Jed shook his head.

'Why?'

'Well, there's Pep's bail money for a start. If I did a runner he'd lose the lot.'

'He'll make that back in no time flogging them snide strides.'

'And anyway, if I did a runner I'd look as guilty as hell, wouldn't I?'

'How does it look if you're locked up?' Archie asked.

Roxanne put her head round the door, interrupting their plans. 'Telephone for you.'

'Did I mention that I'd love to shag her?' Jed heard Omo ask as he went out to the phone.

'Hello?'

'Jed, it's Lucy.' She sounded as if she had been crying.

'Lucy! Hi. How are you?'

'Oh, Jed, it's awful. Nothing's being done. I went to see the policeman today, McClusky. He told me you were the prime suspect.'

'Oh.' Jed felt a surge of anger. 'That was nice of him.'

'Oh, I didn't take any notice of him. But we ended up shouting at each other and . . . I just needed to talk to someone. I didn't want to bother you. I know you've got your own troubles, but I rang Warren, and he wasn't in, and—' Her misery overcame her and she started to cry.

'It's not a problem, Lucy, really. I'm glad you called. It's good to hear your voice. Why don't I come up to London tomorrow and see you?'

'Oh Jed, that would be so lovely. Are you sure you can spare the time?'

'Of course I can. It'll give me an excuse to get the bike out. I'll see you tomorrow. Bye.' He hung up, feeling a mixture of sadness for Lucy's low spirits and excitement at the possibility of their getting it together this time.

The next day he was all leathered up and sitting astride the bike, ready to go at the same time as the others were leaving for the station.

'Why don't you leave that here?' Archie gestured to the bike. 'Get the train with us. Have a bevvy.'

'I'll get to London quicker on this, and I've got to be back to check in to the cop shop at six.'

'A bit like *The Fugitive*, isn't it?' Bobby said.

'Oh, aye,' Omo agreed, 'where they're chasing him and he's chasing the gadgie with one arm.'

Jed started up the bike. 'If you see Pep before I get a chance to talk to him, tell him I'll be calling to say thank you.'

'Will do,' Archie nodded.

'Sorry about all of this.' Jed looked round at all of them.

'Nae bother, son,' Archie assured him. 'I've enjoyed it. It's been exciting. I'm sorry it's finished in a way.'

'It's far from finished,' Jed said. 'I've got to find out who it was that stitched me up, and why.'

'He never had a motorbike, did he?' Walter said. 'That bloke in *The Fugitive*?'

'Couldn't ride one with just the one arm,' Omo said, 'could he?'

'No, not the baddie.' Walter shook his head. 'The fugitive. What was his name again? Brian something?'

As they all racked their brains, Archie turned to Jed. 'You'd better go. This one could be an all-day job!' As Jed throttled up the engine the throaty growl drowned all conversation. He pulled on his helmet. 'See you on the big river, kid.'

Jed gave Archie the thumbs up and rode off as the guys picked up their kit. 'Richard!' Bobby exclaimed. 'Richard summat.'

'Richard Crenna?' Walter suggested.

'No,' Omo chipped in. 'He was the Hulk.'

'No,' Young Paul suggested. 'That was Bill Bixby.'

It felt good to be on the Triumph, flying down the fast lane of the motorway. It felt like an escape from all his worries and Jed kept his eyes on the road, not noticing the police car pulling out and tailing him. Inside the car two bored patrolmen made an arbitrary decision to pull him over. One of them hit the siren while the other called in the bike's registration over the radio.

His heart sinking once again, Jed pulled over and lifted his visor, waiting for the two policemen to walk over to him, hoping he could keep the helmet on and avoid recognition.

'Going a bit fast there, weren't you?' the first man suggested, and Jed shook his head.

'Take your crash helmet off,' the second man instructed.

'Why?' Jed asked.

'Because I'm telling you to.'

The radio in the patrol car suddenly blared into life: 'Vehicle registered to Jed Shepperd. Keeper currently subject to certain travel restrictions as conditions of bail order . . .'

'Mr Shepperd,' the first policeman said grimly, 'I'm arresting you . . .'

'What for?' Jed shouted.

'. . . on suspicion of breaking your bail condition. We'll have that helmet off now, please.'

As the policeman moved towards Jed, his colleague went behind him, making a grab for the helmet. Jed instinctively recoiled, jerking his

72

head back and smashing the helmet into the face of the man behind him, sending him crashing to the floor. Jed spun round and saw the policeman beginning to struggle to his feet. Blood gushed from his nose.

The following day Jed was back in court, standing in the dock with a cut lip, flanked by two court policemen, listening to the same magistrate as before. 'Mr Shepperd, regarding your failing to comply with the conditions of bail, your explanation, once it can be verified, will be given due consideration by the court. However, the charges of resisting arrest and assaulting a police officer' – he looked across at the two arresting officers who were also in court, one sporting a painful looking swollen nose and black eye – 'two police officers, in fact, in the execution of their duty, the court finds you guilty as charged. Sentence is twenty-eight days in prison. I suggest you go there and cool down!' In the gallery the gutter press leapt to their feet and scrambled for the phones, with Ted Quimby fighting his way to the front.

CHAPTER SEVEN

T wo guards led Jed and a dozen or so other new prisoners to their cells, handcuffed together in pairs. Jed was attached to Jo-Jo, a silent mountain of surly black muscle. Cat-calls rang out from behind closed doors as they passed.

'Yo, Jed!'

'Pop star!'

'Give us a song, son!'

The attention seemed to make Jo-Jo even angrier and he scowled at Jed as if about to beat him to a pulp.

'It's not often we get a celebrity in here,' the first guard commented cheerfully. 'The odd smack-head aristo, but not your actual pop star.' He stopped outside a cell and opened the door. Inside were a pair of bunks and a single bed. On the bed sat an elderly black man, playing a harmonica. To Jed's relief the guard undid Jo-Jo's handcuffs and said, 'In you go.' As Jo-Jo ambled through the door the guard nodded to Jed. 'You too.'

'Here you go, Gentle,' the second guard said to the old man, 'your very own pop star, all the way from Geordieland.'

The door slammed shut behind them. Jed stood

still in the tiny room, not knowing what to do. There was hardly any air and what there was was heavy with tension. 'Hey, man,' Gentle said, his face breaking into a broad smile, 'how's the outside world?'

'Weather's lousy,' Jed commented.

'No shit!' Gentle let out a rumble of laughter and held out his hand. 'I'm Gentle, man.'

'I'm Jed.' He shook the hand. 'Jed Shepperd.'

'I know who you are. We're allowed radios in here, you know.' He turned to Jo-Jo. 'You back again, son?' Jo-Jo gave no indication of having heard, and climbed onto the lower bunk, obviously familiar with the layout. 'That down there's Jo-Jo,' said Gentle. Jed nodded but Jo-Jo just stared back, his eyes showing no emotion. 'What you doing in here, Jed? You're a long way from home.'

'I got arrested for jumping bail, and in the process I chinned a copper.'

'What was you on bail for?'

'Possessing a pound of cocaine, but it wasn't mine.'

Jo-Jo spoke for the first time. 'We'd better call the governor's office.' His sarcasm was quiet and unkind. 'Let him know there's an innocent man down here.'

'Don't pay no mind to him, Jed,' Gentle said. 'He's got a problem with the whole wide world.'

'Careful what you're sayin', old man,' Jo-Jo growled.

Jed pulled back a blanket on the upper bunk and a cockroach, alarmed by the sudden light, scuttled away as he climbed up. 'Rock star,' Jo-Jo murmured contemptuously, 'no shit!'

That night, as the darkness arrived, Jed was still lying on the bunk staring at the ceiling when a lone voice, clear and unaccompanied, started to sing the Lord's Prayer: 'Our Father, who art in heaven, hallowed be thy name, thy kingdom come. . .'

As the beautiful voice echoed round the prison everyone remained silent, each lost in his own private world. '. . . For thine is the kingdom, the power and the glory, for ever and ever. Amen.' It even seemed to have found a chink in Jo-Jo's emotional armour plating. Jed felt physically sick with misery and loneliness.

Pep was also feeling physically sick, but for different reasons. 'I knew it was a bad idea,' he ranted at Emma, 'but you, you went on and on about it, didn't you?'

'I'm sorry, Pep. It's not like Jed to run away from anything.'

'He's run away from *everything*.' The last thing Pep wanted to hear was a character reference for the man who had just lost him a hundred grand. 'First from his home, then from his responsibilities. Now from the police. All my money, gone! Because your brother' – his voice rose to a hysterical pitch – 'your brother didn't have the bottle to face the music. The spineless, rotten bastard!'

'They didn't say you'd definitely lose the

money.' Emma tried to reason with him before he lost control of his temper, with the usual consequences. 'They said it was only a possibility at this stage—'

Pep banged the wall in his fury and Emma edged towards the door. 'Where do you think you're going?' he shrieked. 'This is your fault, isn't it?'

Outside the room, Beckie crouched at the top of the stairs, her head resting between two banisters, her face frightened as she listened to another beating.

'Isn't it?' Pep's voice punctuated the punches. 'Isn't it?'

Bowles, McClusky and Connors stood on the top level of a tall, ugly, multi-storey car park overlooking the Houses of Parliament. 'So,' said Bowles smirking, 'Jed Shepperd isn't gonna be around for a while to stick his crusading nose into all of this. Pity.'

'The Wiltshire police are convinced that he's been sticking his crusading nose in the old Peruvian marching powder,' said Connors, proud of his joke.

'Well done, Charlie,' Bowles said to McClusky, 'and congratulations. It would seem that we've gotten away with murder, literally.'

'You're not out of the woods yet,' McClusky warned. 'What about Adrian Lynn's sister? I had her down at the nick the other day, off her bloody head, shouting and screaming.'

'She's one determined girl,' Bowles said admiringly.

'She could turn out to be a bigger handful than Shepperd,' McClusky said.

'I'll take care of Lucy.' Bowles' tone suggested the topic was closed. 'And by the way, it's "*we* aren't out of the woods yet", not "*you*". You were there too, remember?' McClusky shivered at the memory. 'Here.' Bowles chucked him an envelope. 'Buy yourself a new magnifying glass.'

He walked off towards his parked car with Connors. 'You're gonna have to take care of Roxanne,' he said. 'She's a flake, unpredictable. You hearing me?'

Connors nodded. He understood perfectly.

Jed sat in the prison yard trying to take in everything that was going on around him. Jo-Jo and some of the other prisoners were pumping weights while Gentle sat up against a wall playing a blues harp. Jed could feel a lot of eyes on him.

'You should be playing in a band,' he told Gentle as the old man finished his tune.

'Got a little bit of a problem getting the gigs, man,' Gentle laughed. 'I used to play. Used to play for keeps, with a band, on the road an' all.'

'Yeah?'

'Had an offer to join the J. Geils Band, permanent.'

'The J. Geils Band!' Jed was impressed. 'Blimey. Are they still going?'

'This was back in eighty-six.'

'Oh, right. So . . . what happened?'

'I got into a fight. Drunk. Killed a guy. Unfortunately for me, he was white. So was the jury – and

79

the trial judge. Lived in here for ten years, now, and I'll probably die in here too.' Jed couldn't think of anything else to say and Gentle went back to blowing his harp.

'So,' Gentle continued, taking up the conversation after its musical interlude, 'they're saying you were moving drugs, and you're saying you wasn't?'

'That's right. And as soon as I get out I'm gonna find out what the hell's been going on. Because whoever it was stitched me up probably had a hand in murdering my mate, and stealing all my money as well.' For a moment Jed became lost in self-pity. 'All that bread. Every penny I'd made. Royalties from the songs I'd written. All gone.'

A sudden crash of weights hitting the floor made him jump and he looked up to see Jo-Jo storming towards him. 'That wasn't your money, man!' Jo-Jo shouted angrily.

'What?'

'They weren't your songs! Where d'you think they come from? All those riffs and all those licks? You think they fell out of the trees or something? Or out of the atmosphere? No, man! You stole that shit! From him' – he pointed to Gentle - 'and me, and every other black man who paid for them over the years, with his tears, and his pain, and his life.'

All eyes were definitely on them now, expecting to have the boredom enlivened with a fight. Even the guards were watching, smiling, enjoying a bit of light relief. Jed said nothing. The moment passed and Jo-Jo went back to his weights.

'He's one bad-tempered person, that Jo-Jo,' Gentle said, 'but there's truth in what he says.' Putting the harp back to his lips he blew a bluesy version of 'The Blaydon Races'.

Studley House was being emptied of all trace of Jed's existence. Roxanne was standing at an upstairs window looking down on the trucks being loaded with furniture and equipment, when she saw a Jaguar pulling into the driveway. The car stopped and two men climbed out. Roxanne watched one of them – the one she had seen at Ade's funeral – ask one of the humpers a question and saw the man point to the house. The two men headed indoors. She instinctively knew that she was the one they were after. She ran downstairs and made for a side door near to the garage block where her Golf GTi was parked.

'Miss!' The humper's shout made her heart leap. 'There's a couple of gentlemen looking for you. I sent them up to . . .' His words were drowned in the roar of the car's engine as she raced off down the drive.

That evening Bowles entertained Lucy to dinner at his apartment. They washed caviare and smoked salmon down with expensive claret and then settled into armchairs. Bowles played seductive music over his system. 'It's terrible,' Lucy said, 'Jed being locked up like this. Can't you do anything, Warren?'

'Not really. And to be honest I'm not sure I'd even want to try.'

'Don't say that.'

'Listen, Lucy. I want to believe he's innocent too. But at the end of the day . . .' He let his words hang in her mind.

'I told you, he was coming up to see me when he got arrested. To try and cheer me up. And as for the drug-dealing, that's just ridiculous.'

'How can you be sure?'

'Because through my brother I met lots of drug-dealers, and he's not like them.'

Bowles sighed, as if even his patience was being tried now. 'What, so everyone else is wrong and Jed is the innocent man? Let's look at this, Lucy. He was, *is*, suspect number one in your brother's murder—'

'Oh, come on, Warren! The police aren't even sure that it *was* murder any more.'

'And then he runs off back to his rock-star house in the country and, coincidentally, the local police find a pound of cocaine in his fridge.'

'I don't believe it.'

'I'm not making it up, Lucy, darling. These are facts.' He thought for a moment. 'No, it just makes too much sense. In trouble with drugs, paying out more and more money. Adrian probably tried to put a stop to it, God love him . . .'

Lucy was finding it hard to maintain her faith against Bowles' plausible arguments. 'They've made a mistake,' she said firmly. 'It wouldn't be the first time, would it? My brother's death was down to someone else. I'm sure of that, and I'm going to help Jed find out who it was. Where to start, though?' The thought of the task ahead was almost overwhelming and she sank her head in her hands. Bowles moved close and put his arm round her.

'You're gonna need to go through all the proper legal channels,' he cooed.

'Then that's what I'll do. I have money.'

'Not that kind.'

'Then I'll get a loan or something. I don't know.'

'How's about I put my team onto it?' he suggested.

'Oh, would you, Warren?'

He smiled. 'It's not you and Jed against the world, you know. I'm in there as well.'

'How can I ever repay a friend like you?' Lucy thought she might be going to cry.

'For you, Lucy, anything.' He dismissed the very idea with a wave of his hand. 'I mean it.'

'Not for me, Warren. For Adrian and for Jed.'

Bowles nodded. 'It is rather wonderful, you know, the way you value the principles involved here. Truth. Justice. Honesty. We're very much alike, you and I.'

'It's more than that, Warren. I want to help Jed get out of this mess, and then maybe I can help him put his life back together. There's no one else around.'

'Taking up where Adrian left off?'

Lucy thought about it. 'Maybe. Any luck on that front?'

'I've spoken to all the management people I know, but as soon as you mention Jed's name they all back off. He's poison, I'm afraid.'

'You did your best.'

'Can't do any less. Adrian instilled that in me all those years ago.'

'You're such a good friend, Warren.'

He gave her a squeeze and she kissed him on the cheek, which wasn't what he had been hoping for. She looked at her watch. 'I'd better go. I'm going to go down and visit Jed, if I can. The banks won't allow me access to any details of Adrian's various business transactions, but maybe Jed could get them to release the info.'

'Maybe.' Bowles nodded slowly.

'I'll keep you informed.'

'Please.' He smiled warmly until she was out of the door.

Then his expression turned to ice.

CHAPTER EIGHT

The guard stopped outside their cell the next morning. 'Shepperd, Collins,' he barked, and Gentle came out, followed by a sleepy Jed.

'Yeah?' Jed said.

'Get your arse in gear,' the guard instructed. 'You're going to work.' Jed didn't ask any questions, but followed Gentle and the guard to a big, cold, concrete workroom full of cons working under the watchful eyes of their guards. 'Said in your details that you used to be an engineer,' the guard said.

'That's right.' Jed looked around him and felt a rush of nostalgia for the years he had spent in a similar workroom with his mates. All his firmest friendships had been forged in a place like this, during a time of certainties and regular routines. It had all seemed so restrictive and onerous at the time, but now he relished the thought of working with his hands again amid the noises and smells of heavy industry.

'You ever seen one of these before?' the guard asked, pointing to a slightly battered but gleaming lathe.

'Oh yes.' Jed ran his hands lovingly over the cold metal of the machine. 'It's been a long time, but I used to be quite an expert in my day.' He made some chuck-key adjustments and started it up. As liquid coolant flowed through the pipes he felt a comfortable glow of contentment.

'Right,' the guard said, handing him some engineering drawings, 'let's see if you can make these.'

'What are they?'

'What's it to you?' the guard snapped aggressively. Jed shrugged, he certainly didn't want to get into a ruck about it. The guard pointed to a stacked pile of metal. 'You've got your raw materials there. I'll be back later, see how you're getting on.'

As the guard walked away Gentle came towards him, sweeping the floor. 'You all right there, guitar man?'

'Righter than I've been for a long time.' Jed gazed at the lathe. 'Boy, this takes me back.'

'Back to where?'

'Back to Newcastle. Full circle. I started out working on a lathe. Now, after everything that's happened to me, all the strange, mad, nutty things, I've ended up here, working on a lathe. It's a funny old life.'

'I say it's a sign, man, that's what I say. You've got somebody looking out for you, Jed. It's a sign, sure enough. Hallelujah!'

'If it's a sign of anything, it's a sign telling me I've been a complete daft twat and I should have listened to that little voice, in there' – he tapped the back of his head – 'and stuck to a proper job.'

'It's a sign from God, I tell you.'

'Ah, that's all bollocks.' He went back to work, not realising how greatly he had offended Gentle.

'Don't say that, man! That's a right wrong thing to be sayin'! The Lord God Almighty isn't bollocks.'

'I don't believe like you do, Gentle. It's that simple.'

'Listen to me, Jed. Everyone believes in a god of some kind, at some time. Ain't no disbelievers on a sinking ship. When you was standing in the dock of that courtroom and you was in trouble, who'd you call on?' He waited only a few seconds for Jed to reply. 'You tellin' me you didn't say a prayer boy? Not even a incy-wincy, tiny little prayer?'

'I might've said a . . . small prayer,' Jed conceded, grudgingly.

'What'd I tell you?'

'But it didn't do me any good, did it? I still ended up in here.'

'Maybe you was meant to come here.'

'Why?'

'Hey, it's not for me to find the answers to all your questions, Jed.'

'Oh, yes, that old chestnut. No answers, no proof, just blind faith. Same old cop-out. How can you believe in anything after everything that's happened to you?'

'What else do you think I have to get me through each an' every day and night?'

A guard suddenly appeared behind Gentle. 'You stoppin' this prisoner from workin', boy?'

'No, sir.' Gentle jumped. 'Just sweeping, sweeping, sweeping.' He went back to his work.

'He wasn't stopping me from—' Jed protested.

'Shut your mouth! I don't recall askin' you to speak!' As the guard strutted off Jed returned his attention to the lathe.

That night he sat on his bunk in the dark, just able to read a scribbled lyric by the tiny shaft of light coming in from the window above. He could hear the other men's steady breathing and began to sing quietly.

God in heaven, hear my plight –
On my darkness shed eternal light.
I am weak but you are strong.
I can't count the times when I've done wrong.
Please forgive me, if you can –
Lord, you know that I'm a troubled man.
Lord, you know that I'm a troubled man.

A low grumbling voice rose from the bunk below. 'You'll be more than a troubled man if I put my hands around your neck! Now shut that noise, you hear?' Jed did as Jo-Jo suggested.

Back in Newcastle, Jed's mates were racking their brains for ways to help him. Archie, Omo and Big Chrissie were holding a meeting outside Archie's shed, while Walter pottered around the next allotment, weeding.

'What about a fighting fund?' Chrissie volunteered.

'What about busting him out?' Omo suggested.

'Don't be daft.' Chrissie slapped him on the top of his head. 'He's only in for a month.'

'Here!' Walter stood up, holding a leek wrapped in an old newspaper, reading the print. 'This paper's saying that Jed killed his manager!'

'It's all right, Walter,' Archie called back. 'Them's old papers you're looking at. Get back to your cabbage.'

'Well, there must be something we can do,' Omo said. 'Whatever he has or hasn't done, he's our mate. We can't just sit here like twats and let him rot in there.'

They were all in agreement, but none of them had any idea what to do. Archie decided to take himself over to Pep's house to talk to Emma.

When he got there the road was full of reporters, photographers and a television news OB van. When they realised he was going to the house they all pounced.

'Who are you?'

'What's your name?'

'Can you get us in there?'

'D'you know Jed Shepperd?'

'Have you got a quote for our readers?'

A pretty female reporter blocked his way. 'Could you give us a comment, please? It's for *News at Six*.' She looked desperate, 'Anything?'

'I could, pet,' Archie said, 'but there might be kiddies watching.' He walked around them to the front door and gave a prearranged knock. The door opened a couple of inches and the press pack surged forward. Archie squeezed through the gap but a reporter managed to get his foot through as well, just in time to get it unceremoniously stamped on. The foot retracted with a scream of pain and the door was slammed shut.

'What a scrum out there!' Archie said, going through to the kitchen with Emma, who had all the papers spread out on the table. They showed mocked-up pictures of Jed as a convict with a number round his neck alongside glossy publicity pictures of him as a popstar. Quimby's 'It's all gone wrong for Geordie Jed' story was stuck on the fridge door.

'Poor Jed,' Emma said. 'Look at him!'

'What's Pep said about all the bail money going down the toilet?' Archie asked.

'Nothing, he's been as good as gold about it.' Emma avoided Archie's eyes, knowing he would know she was lying.

'If there's anything we can do for Jed, or for you, you only need say the word, you know.' She looked at him as if she didn't know what he meant and his eyes travelled to the bruises on her arms. She tried to cover them up. 'Why do you put up with it?'

'What?'

'Come on Emma – Pep!'

'We're getting married, Archie,' she burst out angrily. 'I'd ask you to remember that while you're in his house.' Archie shook his head, giving up on it, and Emma tried to change the subject, indicating the papers. 'The whole world must know about this. It's terrible. I hope to God they've all gone before Pep gets home.'

'Hello?' A woman's voice came in through the letterbox. 'Is Emma there please?'

'Bugger off and leave us alone, will you?' Emma screamed.

'No,' the voice persisted, 'I'm not from the newspapers. I'm a friend of your brother's, sort of.'

'Sort of?' Archie asked as he and Emma made their way out to the hall, bending down to talk to the voice.

'Yes. You see, I met Jed when I was in Wiltshire. I was down there at a record fair. That's what I do, you see, buy and sell old records. And Jed gave me his phone number, but then my bag was stolen and . . . oh, dreadful business! Anyway, I'm going down there again in a few days and I'd like to go and see him. If I can.'

Emma looked at Archie and they both made a simultaneous decision, opening the door just long enough for her to dash in. 'Hello,' the woman panted as they slammed the door behind her. 'I'm Wendy.'

When Roxanne went to visit Jed in prison, the guard wouldn't even let him clean himself up. 'You look terrible,' she said, the moment she saw him through the thick glass screen.

'Never mind that – it never was a pretty sight. Any news?'

'Jed' – she took a deep breath – 'you were set up and it wasn't right. They are going to hurt you. I couldn't sit back and do nothing.'

'They? Who are they?'

Roxanne averted her eyes, unable to look at him. She seemed frightened. 'I can't say, Jed, but I've spoken to the police and when you get out of here it's going to be over.'

'What do you mean?' Jed asked. 'What have you done?'

'I told them those drugs were mine.'

'But they weren't!' He thought for a second. 'Were they?'

'I told them I was a heavy user, and that I'd bought the blow and was keeping it in your house. I told them you knew nothing.'

'But you'll go to prison,' Jed protested, 'for a long time.'

She shook her head. 'My father is a senior diplomat with the German government here. So I'm to be deported. No more. To save a scandal back home.'

'But they weren't your drugs, were they?'

'You'll be out of here soon, Jed. That's all that matters. And you'll never see me again. I'm sorry about all of this.'

'Who set me up, Roxanne? If you know you have to tell me.'

'I can't, Jed, I'm too frightened. It's too dangerous now. I have to go. They may already know I'm here.' She stood up to leave.

'Who, Roxanne? Who? Wait a minute!' As she walked away he somehow knew that he would never see her again.

'Roxanne!' he shouted at her departing back.

The next day Jed was already packed and waiting

when the guard arrived at his cell door. 'Shepperd? Got your kit together?'

'Get out, boy,' Gentle told him. 'You've done your time.'

'Thanks.' Jed held out his hand.

'For what?'

'I'm not sure, but thanks.' They shook.

'Don't be tryin' any of that hand-shakin' shit on me, man,' Jo-Jo growled. Jed nodded and made for the door.

'Stay angry, Jed,' Gentle called after him. 'It's the only way you'll ever find out what happened. As soon as you relax, you lose.'

'Gonna be makin' any more records?' the guard asked as they crossed the courtyard to the main gates.

'God knows!'

In the plain, unfriendly reception area Wendy waited with half a dozen other people. Occasionally she glanced at the young woman next to her, who was looking nervously around the room.

'Boyfriend is it?' Wendy asked her.

'Kind of. What about you?'

'Someone very special.' Wendy glowed.

The woman nodded. 'It's so rare that you meet a person nowadays that you really connect with.'

'That's exactly how I feel. When I first met . . . you know.' Wendy gestured towards the prison. 'I just knew. You do, don't you?' Her companion nodded. 'Where's he from?'

'Up north.'

Wendy smiled. 'That's a coincidence, so is he.'

'Really? Whereabouts exactly?'

'Newcastle,' Wendy said. 'He's a singer.'

'So is he,' said the other woman. 'By the way, my name's Luc—' But at that moment Jed walked in through the door, giving a puzzled smile as he saw them both waiting.

As the three of them emerged into the daylight, a crowd of reporters and snappers were waiting for them, including Ted Quimby. As they rushed forward with their cameras flashing and shouted questions, the frightened trio scurried for a taxi.

'Jed!' Quimby shouted after him. 'Ted Quimby. Any comment for your fans? Who are the girls, Jed? How does it feel to be free, Jed?' As the taxi took off the photographers ran alongside still firing off frames. Their pictures had to be got quickly, in time for the evening editions.

The same shot made it onto the front page of the first paper Warren Bowles saw. The jubilant headline was FREE AS A BIRD.

'Free as a bird,' Bowles snarled, throwing the paper down angrily, 'and dead as a dodo.'

CHAPTER NINE

From Wendy's window the waters at the mouth of the Tyne looked choppy and uninviting. The view was a long way from the gentle, rolling hills of Wiltshire. Jed was strumming on his guitar, trying to give shape to an idea, when Wendy came back into the room.

'How does it feel, then?' she asked.

'Being back? It's not exactly "hail the conquering hero", is it?'

'You sure you don't want to come to Hamburg? These Euro vinyl marts can be fun.'

'No thanks.'

'If it's a money thing, Jed, don't worry — I can pay.'

'It's not a money thing. I've got bread. I borrowed some off my sister. I appreciate the offer but I've got stuff to sort out. I've got to find some kind of a job for a start.'

'A music-type job?'

'It's the only thing I know, other than working a lathe, and there's not much call for that any more.' He strummed a few notes on the guitar. 'I'll find something.'

'What if you don't?' Wendy asked doubtfully. 'What then?'

'Then . . . I'll starve, or I'll rob, but one way or another I'm gonna get my life back on track. Get myself somewhere to live and then set about finding Roxanne. She's the key to all of this.'

'I'll keep an eye out for her while I'm over there, but don't hold your breath. Germany's a big country.' She passed him a key. 'For the front door. You can look after it while I'm away.' She paused for a second. 'Or longer, if you want.'

'Thanks Wendy.' He smiled. 'But . . . can we just take it slowly?'

She nodded. 'It might be a good thing to try and forget about all that's happened in the last few months, you know?'

'Come again?'

'Well, wallowing in self-pity and all that . . .'

'Self-pity?' he exploded. 'I got stitched up and then I got locked up, and somebody topped my manager! I can hardly just forget about it! And I'm not going to. I don't want to.' He hit a chord and twanged a string. 'Aw, shit!'

'Well then, make use of your present state of mind.'

'How? Suicide?'

'Songs. Channel it all into the songs. The best ones always come out of adversity.'

'What do you think I'm trying to do?' he asked, exasperated and annoyed at having to change a string. 'But songs about how the big daft Geordie got stitched up and ripped off? I can't see that setting the record racks on fire.'

'Depends how well it's done. It worked all right for Sting.'

96

'Yeah,' he conceded, 'but he's a sex-god, albeit an ageing and balding one. I'm sorry, Wendy. I just need to be on my own for a while. I don't want to be with—'

'Me?'

'Anybody.'

'My uncle's got a cottage on Holy Island. Never used it. If you want to be—'

'Back in solitary confinement? No thanks. I just want to wander around the town again. Get me bearings. You know?'

'Well, the cottage is there if you want it. Key's behind the bedroom clock.'

'I must seem like one really ungrateful bastard,' he said. Wendy smiled a sexy and forgiving affirmative. 'I'm not.'

She nodded understandingly. 'I've got to get the tickets by six or else the price goes up. Sure you don't want to come? Going . . . going . . .'

'Positive.'

'. . . gone.'

'We'll go out for a meal when you get back, though,' he said as she headed for the door. 'Somewhere special.'

'It's a date.' She smiled and kissed him, leaving him to fix his broken guitar string.

As he watched her go from the window he began to sing: 'Still I dream of it, of that happy day when I can say I've fallen in love, and it haunts me now, like a dream that's somehow linked to all the stars above . . .'

As her car disappeared from view he felt suddenly sad, why couldn't he settle down and marry

a girl like that? Someone kind, caring and understanding? Picking up his guitar he raised it above
his head, about to smash it to the floor in frustration, like the pop stars of his youth. But something held him back from destroying it and he put
it down gently. It was time to think of rebuilding
his life, not breaking it up even further. The first
problem was money, which meant finding a job.

The next day he went to the job centre, but the
pen-pusher he had to queue to see just wanted
an autograph. Jed strode out in disgust and made
his way to a café in the city centre where he sat
down to study the situations-vacant column of
the local paper. There was nothing there for him
either, so he headed for the Legion bar in search
of company.

'Do you know Sid Flynn?' Archie asked him.

'No.'

'Scrap man. Bit of a piss artist, but a canny
bloke. I heard he was looking for a feller.'

'Working in a scrapyard?' Had things really
come to this?

'It's cash in hand,' Archie said, 'and Sid's
always out on the gargle so you'd be left to your
own devices pretty much. And . . .' He trailed off.

'What?'

'Well' – Archie looked a little nervous – 'I know
you're a proud one, son, but beggars and choosers,
you know.'

'And a bird in the hand's better than a poke in
the eye with a big stick?'

'Something like that.'

'Where abouts is he?'

Archie's directions took Jed out of town on a long, pitted dirt road running parallel to the river, past run-down auto body repair shops and builders' yards. Every few steps the tarmac had collapsed, forming huge craters, which meant no bus could manage the route. Big metal gates guarded the scrapyard and above them was the legend 'Flynn's Exotic Metals'. Inside the yard hard-looking men were cutting up cars with oxy-acetylene torches, burning the outer rubbers from lengths of copper cable and lifting auto wrecks into the crusher with an electromagnetic crane grab. A mongrel, its tail looped in a circle, chased around looking for rats. A Mercedes 380 SEL was parked outside a Portakabin in the corner of the yard and inside Jed found the man he took to be Sid Flynn. Flynn was in his mid-fifties and his red face bore witness to the amount of whisky he consumed in an average working day. The success of the yard showed in his sheepskin jacket, gold bracelets and half-sovereign pinkie rings. He shared the Portakabin with a menacing Rottweiler bitch he called Major.

'It'll be worth the money for the novelty value,' Flynn laughed when he found out Jed wanted a job, 'having a bona fide pop star working in me yard.'

'I'd appreciate it if the whole wide world didn't get to know about this,' Jed said.

'Your secret'll be safe with me, son. Archie said that you were shipwrecked. Easy come, easy go, eh?'

'Something like that. I've got to go. I'll see you in the morning, then. And thanks.'

Flynn punched him painfully on the shoulder in what was meant to be fun, and grinned. 'Nice easy job to start off with, eh? And bugger what the rest o' them say.' Jed nodded and headed towards the gates and the long slog back. 'Say hello to Archie for us, eh?' Flynn called.

The moment he got back inside the Portakabin Flynn was on the phone, a half empty bottle of Scotch standing on the desk beside a grimy tumbler. 'Charlie,' he said when the phone was picked up, 'you'll never guess what . . .'

Lucy was sitting in the middle of piles of work when Jed called her.

'Hi, it's Jed.'

'Oh, hi, Jed. We were just talking about you.'

'Who's we?'

'Warren's here, Warren Bowles. You remember Warren?' She glanced up at Bowles.

'Oh, yeah, the rich geezer.'

'That's right. Warren thinks you might be able to take on the banks and charge them with negligence.'

'More lawyers no doubt.' Jed raised an eyebrow. 'That would be fun.'

'And he's been putting out feelers on your behalf for potential managers. Do you want to have a word with him?' Bowles shook his head and gestured that he should leave. Lucy signalled for him to stay.

'No, thank you.' Jed sounded tense, she thought,

perhaps annoyed that they should be doing things without asking him first. 'I appreciate his trying to help, Lucy, but it's you I need to talk to. We need to find Roxanne.'

'Where is she?'

'Somewhere in Germany, I think.'

'How are you going to find her?'

'I'd prefer not to go into it over the phone. Could we possibly meet up?'

'I'd like that, Jed. Where are you?'

'Tynemouth.'

'Do you have a number there?' Bowles handed her a piece of paper and a pencil, smiling sweetly. Lucy scribbled down the number. 'All right. Talk soon, Jed. Take care.'

'What's he up to then, our Jed?' Bowles asked casually as he made his way to the front door of Lucy's flat.

'He's going to try and trace Roxanne, the German girl who used to work for him. She visited him in prison and then she vanished.'

'I wonder why he wants to see her again.'

'According to Jed, she knows who set him up.'

Bowles looked surprised. 'Really? Does he have any idea where this Roxanne might be?'

'Somewhere in Germany. But if she's there, I'll find her.'

'You?'

'Well, Jed can't go over there. He's broke.'

'Why don't you let me look into it? I know a lot of people out there.'

'That's sweet of you, Warren, but you've done enough already.'

Bowles could see she was adamant and changed his tack. 'When do you plan—?'

'As soon as possible.'

Bowles nodded as she opened the door for him. 'We still on for dinner tonight?'

'Oh shit! I'd forgotten all about it. Could I pass on it, Warren? I'm knee-deep in work, and I have to go through the details of Adrian's estate.'

'Of course. No problem. I did have a bit of a surprise lined up for you, but what the hell! It'll keep.'

'Oh Warren, if only everyone was as understanding as you.' She proffered a cheek, which he kissed.

But his pretence of warmth and understanding dropped the moment he entered the lift and the doors closed. He pulled out his mobile phone and punched the keys. 'Connors?' he snapped. 'It's me. Pack a bag. You're going to Germany.'

Ted Quimby had decided to hunt without the rest of the pack. His editor had assigned Matt Ford, a hungry young freelance photographer, to him and the pair of them were heading back up to Newcastle in a Toyota Landcruiser with the intention of getting an exclusive story from any source they could bribe, blackmail or seduce.

'So,' Matt said as Quimby reclined beside him in the passenger seat, 'what's the plan, then? I take it there is one.'

Quimby pulled a printout from his pocket and grinned smugly. 'I got this from a friend at the Met. Got the names and addresses of all Shepperd's mates.'

'And you reckon they're gonna talk to you?' Matt was not overly impressed.

'Of course they'll talk to me,' Quimby said patronisingly. 'It's my home town.'

'You're from Newcastle?' Matt didn't believe him.

'Yes. Left when I was four, but they're not to know that, are they?' Matt shrugged. 'I hate it up north.' Quimby shivered. 'Cold, dark, wet, all that "salt-of-the-earth" crap.'

'Think of the per diems, mate.'

'Hmm . . .'

'And the babes! They're anybody's for a bowl of dog food and a half of lager. And we're on expenses.'

'True . . .' Quimby thought for a moment before closing his eyes. 'But I still hate it.'

CHAPTER TEN

Jed was in the crane cab, operating the electromagnet to pick up a scrap car body and dump it into the crusher, when Flynn's Mercedes pulled into the yard. Flynn and four other guys stumbled out, already drunk and merry, and lurched towards the Portakabin, after having a good squint at Flynn's captive pop star. A few minutes later Flynn came back out and waved to Jed, beckoning him over. Jed reluctantly killed the crane's engine, climbed down from the cab and headed for the Portakabin. Inside, the men were all drinking and lounging around. Major was napping in the corner.

'Here he is,' Flynn announced. 'What did I tell you? Have a sit down, son.'

'I'd rather get back to work,' Jed said politely, sensing that things were about to go wrong.

'Ah, howway, now, Jed,' one of the men said, 'play the white man. We've come a long way to see you.'

One of the other men pulled out a camera and flashed it in Jed's face. He looked angrily at Flynn. 'I asked you not to let anyone know.'

'These are me mates,' Flynn protested.

As Jed headed for the door another of the men

shouted after him. 'Hold on, Jed, we're gonna have a little singsong next.'

'I'm not a performing seal, pal.' He made a powerful effort to keep his temper in check. 'You want to sing, then sing on your own.'

'You walk out that door,' Flynn raged, deeply embarrassed to be humiliated in front of his mates, 'and you can just keep on walking.' Jed didn't turn round. 'Ungrateful bastard!'

Once he was outside, Jed's temper began to well within him. He strode over to the crane cab to grab his jacket, but by the time he got there the anger was bubbling almost palpably through his veins. Climbing inside, he started the engine.

Inside the Portakabin, Flynn and his mates were deep into a chorus of 'Crocodile Shoes' when Flynn's Mercedes sailed past the window and dropped neatly into the crusher. Jed was out of the crane cab and leaving the gates by the time Flynn emerged from the Portakabin with the dog, both of them boiling with rage.

'Kill! Kill, Major,' Flynn screamed hysterically. 'Eat the bloody bastard!' Jed started running and disappeared from sight as Major crashed against the gates, foaming at the mouth and contorting herself in paroxysms of fury.

When Jed arrived back at Wendy's house, a Landcruiser was parked outside by the kerb and Quimby jumped out as soon as he spotted him. 'Hello, Jed. Remember me?'

Jed stared at him hard. 'Are you that twat that jumped me outside the nick?'

'You remembered.' Quimby looked pleased. 'I'm touched, Jed.'

Jed kept walking with Quimby running along beside him. 'Quim . . . something or other, wasn't it?'

'Quimby, Jed. How are you?'

'On top of the world.'

'C'mon, Jed, I know your situation. It would be beneficial to both of us if I were to get your side of the story.'

'What story?'

'Your life story, Jed. There'd be a substantial amount of compensation should you grant us an exclusive. And from what I can gather, you need the dosh. Got to be worth discussing over a drink, eh?'

Jed decided to go along with him, at least for the moment. The guy with Quimby – probably a paparazzo, Jed thought – stayed in the car park outside as Jed led Quimby into a café and ordered cups of tea.

'This wasn't exactly the kind of drink I had in mind,' Quimby grumbled, 'but not to worry. Do you take sugar, Jed?'

'Off the record?' Quimby didn't react to the sarcasm and let Jed sort out his own sugar.

'Must be nice to be out. Is it?' Quimby asked, conversationally.

'It's lovely. So pretty here, don't you think?'

'Out of the nick, Jed. The big house. Out of prison.'

'That would be the story? "Jed Shepperd – My Life Behind Bars"?'

'It could be worse. It could be "Jed Shepperd – *His* Life Behind Bars", from an unknown informant.'

'I wonder who that would be. That's the option is it? I tell you all or else you make it up and print it anyway?'

'Today it's the news,' Quimby said breezily, 'tomorrow it's your fish-and-chip wrappers. You'll walk away with thirty grand. Y'gonna tell me you don't need it?'

Jed couldn't deny that he needed money. 'If I said yes – and I haven't yet – what would you want to talk about?'

'Salisbury Prison for starters. It must have got a bit heavy in there. How was it for a pop star in with a load of hardened criminals?' Jed looked bemused. 'I mean, they must have tried to . . . take advantage? Pushed it a bit?'

'They were really good blokes.' Jed shook his head. 'By and large.'

'But maximum-security prison, Jed. A lot of man-to-man marking, I gather. In terms of sex action.'

'Not that I noticed.'

'C'mon, Jed.' Quimby was becoming exasperated by Jed's playing dumb.

Jed thought for a second and decided to throw Quimby a scrap. 'In my cell was a guy doing life, for murder. Been in there ten years. He'll probably die in there.'

'Murderers dying in prison. This is more like it. Don't suppose he was a black feller?'

'He was, as it happens.'

108

'Great!'

'But it's a funny thing . . .'

'Yeah? What?'

'This guy had more dignity, more integrity, more compassion than any man I've ever met.'

Quimby stared at Jed for a moment. 'How wonderful. And don't think I don't sympathise. But what we're after here is a little more . . . basic.'

'How about the story of how Jed Shepperd was framed? How he was set up, and then stitched up, by the police and others unknown?'

'Dodgy ground if you can't prove it. Major law suits and what have you. And it looks bad, knocking our boys in blue. Can you prove it?'

'Not yet. But with a little bit of help I might be able to.'

'Tell you what. You give me an exclusive and I'll look into your claims regarding the police. How's that?'

'How do I know you'll do it?'

'I'll give you my word, as a journalist.' Jed burst out laughing and Quimby looked genuinely upset. 'Don't be too hasty to judge, Jed. I wasn't always peddling sensationalist tabloid crap.' Jed pondered for a few minutes but Quimby was anxious to press on. 'Gimme some sex, Jed. That's what the readers want to read about. "My Prison Gang-Rape Nightmare", or something on those lines.'

'The readers?' Jed asked. 'Or the editors?'

'For fifty grand, who cares?'

'Fifty thousand now?' Jed looked shocked by

the sum and Quimby felt his confidence rising. He pulled out a standard-issue contract.

'I'll just need your moniker on this . . .'

'I could really use the money . . .' Jed made a show of looking thoughtfully at the paper. 'But I'd much rather you stuck it up your arse.' He stood up and walked, leaving Quimby looking shocked and upset. As he came out the photographer started snapping him, not bothering to conceal himself, following him along the street as he went. Jed looked at him and shook his head. 'Can't you find anything better than me to take photographs of?'

'Loads of things.' The photographer kept shooting. 'But you're the only on-his-arse pop star.' For a second Jed wanted to punch him, but he controlled himself. He knew exactly what the guy was trying to achieve.

These hacks were not about to give up, Jed realised, just because he had said no.

When he came out of a bar later in the day with Archie and Omo, the paparazzo leapt out from nowhere and started shooting off flashes in their faces, making passers-by stare. Jed walked off without speaking and Archie and Omo followed. Quimby and his pal jumped into the Landcruiser and glided along behind them. They seemed determined to elicit some sort of reaction.

When Wendy arrived back from Germany Jed took her down to the fish-and-chip shop for a bite to eat. 'I promised you something special,' he said. 'Best fish and chips on the coast. It's funny the things you miss when you're all of a sudden not allowed to have them.'

A young girl came over to them. 'Is he pointing at you?' She gestured at the window. Jed turned to see Quimby outside, waving to him.

'I'm going to end up punching him.'

'That's just what they want you to do,' Wendy warned him. 'A great story for no money.'

'I know, I know. It wouldn't half make me feel good, though.' As they left the chippie Jed snarled at the reporter but walked on by. The pair followed them for a while, taking more pictures, but then decided to let them go. Perhaps they had got the message at last – or were maybe thinking it was time to try a different tack.

In Hamburg, Roxanne was going home to her apartment. As she opened the door the place was in darkness and she switched on the lights. Nothing happened. '*Sheise*,' she hissed and made her way across to the fuse box. As she turned the corner she walked straight into Connors.

CHAPTER ELEVEN

'Archie? Archie Tate?' The man in the suit had to shout to make himself heard over the screams of the lathe.

'Who's asking?' Archie asked, assuming the man was from the Department of Social Security.

'Couple of questions, if I may?' The man came further into the shed.

'This is just hobby, you know' – Archie gestured at the lathe – 'just to keep me hand in, like, for when the good times come again. If a job came up I'd be available.'

'I know times are tough, Archie. That's why I'm here. I want to make you an offer.'

'What kind of an offer?'

The man introduced himself as Ted Quimby, a journalist, but the next thing he knew he was being propelled out of the shed, landing hard on the ground. He instantly sprang back onto his feet. That sort, thought Archie, must have had years of experience of being thrown out of places.

'I'm not interested,' Archie shouted, 'not for any amount of money.'

'If you don't talk to me then someone else will.'

Archie had a large spanner in his hand. 'That may be true where you come from, son, but around here we see things a bit differently. You have to live with the consequences of your actions, you see.'

'I could talk to the DSS about all this.' Quimby nodded back towards the shed.

'That's right, you could.' Archie weighed the spanner in his hand.

'Are you threatening me?'

Archie shook his head. 'It's like this. I've got no work, I sign the dole. If I get banged up, I've got no bills.' He smiled. 'See?' He raised the spanner a little higher. 'Time you were leaving, pal.'

'If you change your mind—'

'I won't.'

'Well, my office will know where I am.' He flicked a business card to Archie and headed off down the road to where Archie could see a bloke with a camera shooting the whole encounter. He stormed back into his shed.

'Three grand's a lot of money,' he muttered, reading Quimby's card.

'You could've got him up from there,' Jed said, coming out from behind the lathe in overalls. 'He offered me fifty.'

'I might ring him back . . .' Archie joked. Jed just smiled, and peered out of the window.

'Has he gone?' he asked.

'Aye. What a way to make a living.'

'They don't do it 'cause they have to. They do it 'cause they like it.' Jed went back to the lathe. 'I appreciate this, Archie.'

'Nae bother, Jed. I owe you one, after that scrapyard carry-on. I don't know how long it'll last, though. Seems there's not the demand for cocktails what there once was.'

Quimby's next stop was the British Legion Club, where he found Bobby – the next on his list - behind the bar. He introduced himself and made Bobby an offer.

'Five grand?' Bobby exclaimed, handing the reporter a beer, 'For what?'

'The inside story.'

'The dirt on Jed, you mean?'

'That's right.' Quimby perched on a barstool.

Bobby shook his head. 'I wish I could tell you some, son. I'd love to take your money, but there isn't any.'

'Come on,' Quimby coaxed, 'he must have told you what went on in prison.'

'Jed's been in prison?' Bobby looked shocked.

'This is a serious cash offer.'

Bobby picked up the beer, reached across the bar and slowly poured it into Quimby's lap. 'And that's a serious dry-cleaning bill.'

Matt was waiting outside as Quimby emerged, walking with his legs apart. 'Couldn't you hold it in?' he asked.

'Shut up,' Quimby grunted, climbing into the Landcruiser, 'and drive to the cemetery.'

'Eight thousand pounds?' Omo exclaimed as he sat beside a gravestone while Big Chrissie loaded leaves onto a trailer hooked up to a small tractor.

Quimby couldn't help noticing that both of them were wearing gold chains and genuine Rolex watches.

'For an hour of your time,' Quimby confirmed.

'Jed's a mate, though,' Omo pointed out.

'I could maybe go to ten.' He could see they weren't biting. 'If you don't talk, someone else will. They'll get all that money.'

'No one's gonna be talking to you about anything,' Big Chrissie told him.

'C'mon boys,' Quimby scoffed, 'this is the real world. Think what blokes like you could do with all that cash.'

A mobile phone bleated and Big Chrissie answered it, walking away from the reporter as he talked. 'Hello, this is Toys for Grown-Ups. What can I do for you?' There was a pause. 'We specialise in them, dual-speed,' he announced proudly. 'No problem. I'll send you a catalogue. Or we have a fax-back line. You fax in your order, you get a stock list by return fax. Delivery's guaranteed within a week.'

'I could maybe go to twelve,' Quimby said, working on Omo, who was now tugging on a spliff.

'It's very quiet here.' Omo cast a bleary eye around the graveyard. 'Very still. Working in a place like this, it gives you time for thinking. Brings home to you the ultimate irrelevance of things material. Money and the suchlike. Twelve grand?' He took a big drag of smoke and shrugged. 'We wouldn't know what to do with it.'

Another mobile phone rang while Chrissie was

still talking. He took it off his belt with his free hand. 'Hello?' he said into the second phone. 'Hang on a minute, I'm on the other line.'

Quimby gave up and walked back to the Landcruiser where Matt was shooting with the long lens. 'What kind of a place is this, where the gravediggers wear Rolex watches, smoke dope and sport two mobile phones?'

'Don't ask me.' Matt shrugged. 'You're the Geordie.'

Bowles was waiting for Lucy at a recording studio, where she was organising an orchestral session, to tell her that Roxanne was dead. 'I'm sorry to hit you with it right at the front of a heavy day,' he said, 'but—'

'No, no, you did the right thing, Warren. Did they say how she died?'

'Drug overdose apparently. I suppose we shouldn't be that surprised. Would you like me to let Jed know?'

'No. I'd like to talk to him, if you don't mind.' Lucy remembered all the people waiting for her in the studio. 'I'd better get in there.' She gave Bowles a hug. 'Thanks for letting me know. I'll ring you tonight.'

'I'll look forward to it.' Bowles watched through the glass as she went back into the studio, shaking his head sadly, playing to the gallery.

At the British Legion Club the guys were holding a council of war. 'He's dangerous,' Bobby announced, 'this bastard. No doubt about it.

117

And he had a snapper with him, taking pictures.'

'He was threatening to shop me to the social,'
Archie agreed.

'He was looking at my medals,' Bobby said. 'If
he finds out I bought them down the quayside,
I'll lose this job.'

'I'm really sorry about all this,' said Jed. He felt
terrible 'Maybe if I wasn't around . . .'

Archie shook his head. 'This is your town,
kidder, not his.'

'We were thinking we could kill him,' Omo
piped up.

Jed burst out laughing, then looked around and
realised that the rest of them were serious. 'You
can't kill him, man. That's . . . murder!'

'Only if they catch you,' Omo pointed out,
'and we've got the perfect place to hide him,
haven't we?'

'Who's ganna think of looking for a body in a
graveyard?' Big Chrissie asked.

'You know,' Archie said thoughtfully, 'it's just
daft enough to work.'

Jed found himself considering it for a second
and quickly came to his senses. 'I don't want this
man killed, all right? I don't want anyone killed. I
can't believe we're sat here even talking about it.'

'We could make him an offer he couldn't
refuse,' Big Chrissie suggested.

'This isn't *The Godfather*, man,' Jed protested.
'I'll think of a way to get rid of him. But in the
meantime, no killing, please.' He went up to the
bar for more drinks.

'We're onto a good thing here,' Big Chrissie
continued. 'Business's booming. I'm not gonna
risk losing it for some tosser from the tabloid
press.'

'So what'll we do?' Archie asked.

'I vote we top him,' Omo said.

'What about the photographer kid?' Bobby
asked.

'Top both of them,' Omo suggested, after a
moment's thought.

'We can't do that, man.' Archie dismissed the
idea. 'Where's it ganna stop?'

'Well, we're gonna have to do something,'
Chrissie said.

'Agreed.' Archie looked over his shoulder at
Jed. 'But let's keep him out the loop. Safer for
everyone.'

Quimby's next target was one Albert Peploe,
known as Pep to his friends, and he and Matt
headed out to the warehouse building where he
operated Hadrian Import/Export Ltd. 'This guy
won't talk for ten grand,' Matt said, 'not when
he's put up a hundred grand to bail Shepperd
out in the first place.'

'That was before Shepperd did a runner,'
Quimby reminded him. 'Maybe Mr Peploe might
just want to talk to get some of his own back.'

Inside, the place was jammed full of electronic
machines, clothes, cigarettes, computer screens
and anonymous packing cases. Quimby found
Peploe in a corner office and knocked on the
door. 'Good morning.'

'What do you want?' Pep was sitting in front of a computer.

'I'm Ted Quimby. I'm a journalist.'

'I know who you are. Big cities are really just small towns. So?'

'I was interested to see that you put up some bail money for Jed Shepperd, before he ran off.'

Pep kept working. 'Were you?'

'Must have left you in a right mess. I wondered if we could talk about it.'

'We just did. Now would you kindly leave?'

'What is it with you lot up here?' Quimby's exasperation got the better of him. 'I'm walking around with fifteen grand in readies for a simple story and everyone's dissing me.'

'Ted,' Pep said, smiling soothingly, 'there's certain people round here that don't exactly love each other. Don't even like each other. But they like your kind even less.' Quimby was taking no notice, looking around at the boxes and merchandise in the warehouse. 'What are you looking for?'

'What exactly do you import, Mr Peploe?'

Pep had had enough. 'Curtis!' he shouted. 'Nigel!' As the two bodyguards ushered Quimby out of the door Pep went back to his computer doodling. Quimby remained silent but made a mental note of everything he could see on the way out.

'Struck out again, did you?' Matt enquired as they drove away under the gaze of Curtis and Nigel.

'Maybe. Maybe not. The bloke who owns this

place puts up a hundred grand to get Jed Shepperd out the nick, and look at it.' He gestured back at the building. 'A dodgy warehouse in the middle of shitsville. Where did all that money come from?'

'Second endowment mortgage?'

'I feel all . . . tingly.' Quimby smiled. 'I can feel those old journalistic juices coming back, starting to flow. I feel' – he considered how he felt for a moment – 'investigative.'

CHAPTER TWELVE

Both Emma and Beckie could tell that Pep's mood was not good when he stormed into the kitchen and poured himself a drink.

'Hi, love.' Emma looked up from giving Beckie her dinner, hoping she might be able to lift his mood if she was jolly enough.

'That's the last thing I need mooching around the factory – a bloody reporter,' Pep mumbled.

'What's that?' Emma wasn't sure if he wanted to talk to her or not.

'We had a visitor at the warehouse today. A journalist. From London, no less! Asking about your good-for-nothing brother.'

Emma gave an involuntary shudder. 'Asking what, exactly?'

'Anything. All sorts. Trying to dig some dirt, I assume. Not that that would be difficult.'

'Did you say anything?'

'You never get it, do you?' He was beginning to refocus his anger onto her. 'You never understand a bloody thing I'm talking about.'

'What?' She just knew what was coming.

'A journalist,' he shouted, 'from London came to the warehouse!'

'Yeah. Asking about Jed.'

'And what did he see?' Pep demanded and Emma shrugged. 'Every bloody thing in there! That's what!' Beckie began to cry as his shouting became more threatening. 'Tell her to shut that crying!'

'Please, Pep, not in front of Beckie.'

Beckie grabbed her Harrods bear as Pep headed for her mother, his last vestiges of control vanishing. Beckie turned and stared, transfixed, tears streaming down her face as Pep laid into Emma. 'I don't want to be embarrassed,' he shouted. 'I don't want any attention. I just want a quiet life! Have you got that?'

Quimby and Matt were waiting for Jed outside the fish-and-chip shop again. 'Any comment on the death of your former personal assistant, Jed?' Quimby asked.

'What?' Jed couldn't think what he meant. 'Who?'

'Roxanne Pallenberg.' Quimby's words made Jed stagger. 'What? You didn't know?' He turned to Matt. 'Get the picture! Get the picture!' Matt pounded the auto-wind as Quimby continued to relentlessly break the news. 'Found dead in her Hamburg apartment. Cause of death given as an overdose of barbiturates.' Jed was near to tears. 'First it was your manager, and now your PA. Bit of a Jonah, aren't you, boy?'

Jed's self-control finally broke and he slammed his fish and chips into Quimby's face, sending him to the ground with the force of the blow as Matt continued to circle round them. When

Jed turned on him, Matt tried to run but Jed caught him within a few seconds, snatching the camera.

'No,' Matt pleaded frantically, 'not the Leica. Please, man. It's an M6!'

'Expensive?' Jed enquired.

'Three grand's worth.'

'Insured, I hope.'

'Oh, yeah, but—' Jed hurled the camera to the ground, where it smashed into pieces. 'You friggin' philistine!'

As Jed looked back across the street he saw Quimby being helped to his feet by a policeman - how did they always manage to be at the wrong place at the wrong time? As Quimby pointed in his direction Jed walked quickly away, ducking down an alley before breaking into a gallop. He zig-zagged through a few streets until he came to a church. The door was open so he let himself in, closing it behind him and sliding the bolt across. He slipped into a pew near to the back, gasping for breath. Some choirboys were practising Fauré's *Requiem*, their beautiful voices echoing round the church. A woman in her mid-thirties sat down beside him. He turned and realised she was the vicar.

'Bit of a surprise, I know,' she said, 'a girl in a dog collar. But people are slowly coming around to it. Have you come to pray?'

Jed shook his head, 'I've come to hide, if that's OK.'

She nodded. 'Would you like to pray now that you're here?'

'I'd like to, 'cause I've just had some really bad news, but I'm not a believer. For me it's simple. You're born, you die, you're dust. The end.'

'You sound very sure of all that.'

'Is there any evidence to make me think otherwise?'

'No, but that's the whole nub of faith. You have to base it on a firm belief and conviction.'

'Blind faith.'

'If you like.'

'Good band.' He indicated the choir and glanced nervously at the door.

'Who are you hiding from?'

'Take your pick.' He sighed. 'Reporters, photographers, policemen.'

'The church has been used many times through the centuries as a sanctuary for the persecuted. Some of them much bigger sinners than you — even bearing your last record in mind.' She smiled. 'Who knows? Maybe a force more powerful than the press guided you in through those doors.'

'Spare me the sermon, would you?' Some of the choirboys had noticed him and he acknowledged them with a wave.

'Fancy joining in? I'm sure the boys would be thrilled.'

'I'm gonna have to go.' He got up.

'If you could spare a little change before you leave us, we'd be thankful. For our appeal.' She pointed to a photo display at the side of the church, and led him over to it. He stared at the photographs of suffering people, lost in his thoughts. 'No matter how bad it gets,' she said, 'or how low you feel, there's always someone, somewhere, worse off than you. Right?'

'I was actually thinking how effective a camera can be in the right hands,' Jed said.

'I don't suppose,' the vicar said, obviously having decided to chance her luck, 'you would consider playing a benefit concert for us? That would be quite a coup.'

'I don't know. I'll think on it.'

'I wish that God had blessed me with a wonderful singing voice. The things I could've done.' She smiled softly. 'I'll leave you to your thoughts.' By the time Jed left the church he was more confused than when he had come in. He needed to get away for a bit.

Holy Island was joined to the mainland by a causeway. Jed's taxi dropped him off on the mainland side and he walked across, asking a local man for directions as he went. Wendy's uncle's stone cottage overlooked the bay, with no other buildings in sight. Jed had brought the key with him but the door was already open. The sparse interior had a lived-in feel to it. The wooden floors had been worn down over the years and an over-stuffed sofa sagged in the middle. There was an old upright piano and many of the family pictures on the walls included Wendy.

Jed dumped his bag and tried a few notes on the piano. He thought for a moment, then sat down and played a bit more. The simple, single notes began to turn themselves into a tune. He sang along for a little while, then stopped. He looked at the keys and shook his head, deciding to make himself a cup of tea instead.

Shepperd's sister, Emma, was next on Quimby's list. He found her watching her daughter play on the swings in the park, and sat down on the bench next to her. She didn't notice Matt shooting pictures from the distance with a new camera, nor, thank God, had she noticed the tiny microphone pinned to Quimby's lapel.

'Emma Shepperd?' Quimby enquired.

'Who's asking?'

'I'm Ted Quimby. I'm a friend of your brother's. I—'

'You're from the papers, aren't you?'

'That's right. I—'

Emma stood up and walked off. 'I don't want to talk about Jed. He specifically asked me not to.'

'I don't want to talk about Jed.' Quimby jumped up and followed her. 'It's Pep I'm interested in. I'm doing a very positive piece about Jed and the North-East, and I was impressed that Pep put so much money on the line, to bail Jed out.'

'It's family. That's what you do.'

'But families have their problems. So I heard.'

'Every family has its problems. Pep's under an awful lot of pressure at the moment. It's understandable he'd—' She seemed to stop herself saying something. Quimby carried on pumping.

'He'd what?' He felt he was nearly there. 'Get upset occasionally? With you?'

'Not just with me, with everything.'

'They're a couple of big lads your Pep has working for him, aren't they?'

'Curtis and Nigel? Yeah, they're bodybuilders.'

'I dare say they could be body-*breakers* if things had to get rough, eh?'

'I dare say.'

'What exactly does Pep do, Emma? What does he deal in? How does he make his money?'

She hesitated for a second, checking that the girl – Beckie, wasn't it? – was playing happily. 'He'd kill me if he knew I was talking to you.'

'This is off the record, Emma,' he assured her. 'Sometimes it's just good to talk to someone.'

Jed had taken a pile of paperwork with him to Holy Island, determined to try to work out what had happened to all the money, but none of it made any sense to him. As he sat on the floor, surrounded by accounts and bank details, he was only peripherally aware of the sound of a car engine. Outside, Lucy's car drew up on the other side of the causeway and parked. As she set off on foot towards the island another car pulled up next to hers and a man got out. He peered inside Lucy's car and then spotted her almost on the island. Going back to his car he opened the boot and pulled out a hunting rifle with a telescopic sight, which was secreted in a golf bag. Jumping up onto Lucy's car he lay across the roof in the firing position, getting Lucy's head in the centre of his sights.

'Bang!' Connors said to himself and gave a nasty little chuckle.

By the time Lucy reached the cottage Jed had given up on the paperwork and was back at the piano. She was shocked by what a mess he looked, unshaven and dishevelled.

'Lucy!' He was surprised to see her.

'Roxanne is dead.'

'I know. I kinda ran off up here to get away from it all. How on earth did you know where I was?'

'I called the number you gave me. The lady who answered gave me this address.'

Jed realised that he hadn't tipped Wendy off not to give his whereabouts away.

'You'd best come in.'

CHAPTER THIRTEEN

Quimby was snoozing on his bed in the Newcastle Hilton when the phone rang. 'Hello?'

'Can I speak to Ted Quimby?' A man's voice.

'This is Quimby. Who's that?'

'This is Archie Tate,' the voice said nervously. 'Listen, I've been thinking about your offer. How much is an exclusive worth?'

Quimby was now wide awake. 'Ten grand. But that's as long as it's everything.'

'Don't worry. It'll be the whole nine yards,' Archie assured him. 'I know things about Jed Shepperd that are . . . well, unprintable, probably.'

'You let me worry about what's printable and what's not,' Quimby reassured him.

'I'll want the money up front.' Archie's voice was trembling. 'The whole lot, for all the dirt.'

'I'm surprised to hear from you.'

'Yeah, well, times are hard. Harder than hard for some.'

'No problem.' Quimby was reassuring, determined not to give Archie any reason to rethink his decision. 'You shouldn't feel bad about it, Archie. People are doing it every day. I was beginning to

131

think you lot weren't human. Now, when and where? Do you want to come over here to the hotel?'

'No.' Archie now sounded very nervous. 'It's got to be somewhere well out of the way. If I'm seen talking to you, I'm a dead man!'

'No problem, Archie.' Quimby scrambled around for a pencil and paper. 'Anywhere you want, mate.' Archie gave him an address. 'Right, see you there.'

'Come alone.'

'Don't worry, I'll be alone. Ta-ra.' He put down the receiver. 'Schmuck,' he muttered, dialling another number. 'Matt? Get your lenses ready – we've got a date.'

'How did you get to know about Roxanne?' Lucy asked as she and Jed strolled along the beach, skimming stones and retreating from the occasional big wave.

'A reporter threw it at me yesterday. Guy from a tabloid. I ended up punching him.'

'Oh, no. Was there a photographer there?'

'Oh yes.' He thought for a second. 'Strange, all this. First Adrian dies, now Roxanne.'

'You don't think it was suicide?'

'I don't know what to think any more. The guy from the tabloid reckoned I was a Jonah. Maybe he was right. You're probably in mortal danger right now just talking to me.'

'Don't be silly,' Lucy said.

'Have the police said anything regarding Adrian?' Jed asked.

'They keep throwing your name at me. But I'm pretty sure they're going to try for an accidental-death verdict at the inquest. Lazy bunch of bastards. To all intents and purposes the case is closed.

'Not for me it's not.'

'Nor me. Paradigm's lawyers informed me that anything and everything Adrian earns posthumously is rightfully theirs.'

'What?'

'Because of your unrecouped advances they're the rightful owners of anything Adrian was involved with.'

'That can't be right. Have you spoken to anyone about it?'

'Warren checked it out.'

'Warren? I don't trust him.'

'You've only met him once, Jed. He's been a big help to me over the last few months. God knows what it would have cost if he hadn't offered to help.'

'How do you mean, "help"?'

'He put his legal team onto it, for free. It was them that found out about Roxanne and he's been busting his arse trying to find you some representation.'

'Nothing in life is free, Lucy. There's always a price to be paid.'

'Yeah.' She looked straight at him. 'But for the moment we're here on the beach. Let's make the most of it.' He smiled and nodded and they walked on. 'I intended to set up a trust fund in memory of Ade, for struggling musicians.'

'That would've been handy,' he said and they both laughed. 'Cup of tea?'

'Good idea.'

Some distance away, Connors watched the scene with interest – his vision more than adequately aided by the lens of his hunting rifle.

Jed and Lucy settled down once more in front of a blazing fire with the paperwork. Lucy handed him some more papers from her bag. 'This is stuff I eventually managed to get from the bank.'

Jed looked at it and shook his head. 'I might as well be reading Swahili!'

'It's all terribly complex, deliberately so, I'm sure, knowing Adrian. This stuff though . . .' She pointed to some figures.

'Incomings and outgoing. Bank transfers.' He read for a few moments. 'Dear me, there was some money! Where did all this go?' He checked some of the figures he already had. 'These don't tally up at all. Here, look. Thirty-seven grand out of this one, but not showing up on any of these.'

'Does it say who it was made out to?'

'No, banker's draft.'

'When was that dated.'

'May seventeenth,' he read.

'Fancy that! My birthday!'

'Really?' Jed smiled and then both of them thought for a moment. 'Really?' he said with a trace of suspicion.

'Oh dear.' Lucy looked worried.

'What?'

'My car was bought on that day. It was a birthday present from Adrian.'

'How much did it—'

'It should have been forty-one thousand and something, but Adrian managed to get a discount . . . for cash.'

'How much was it?'

Lucy wished the floor would open up and swallow her, 'Thirty-seven thousand. Exactly.' They sat in horrified silence for a few moments. 'See if there's one for last year for' – she hesitated for a second – 'forty-five thousand.'

Jed checked the audit columns. 'July twenty-eighth.' he said, 'banker's draft again.'

Lucy was appalled. 'That was the deposit on my apartment. He insisted. Oh, Jed . . .'

'I've not paid the tax on that money yet!' He gave a deep sigh. 'Never mind. At least I know where it went. I'm gonna have to get these figures checked out by an expert.'

'Why don't you let me take care of that?' He looked at her dubiously. 'Please, Jed. It's important for me that you trust me.'

He studied her for a moment, then quickly said, 'I want to play you something.' He pulled a cassette from his shirt pocket.

'Great. New songs?'

'No.' He slotted the tape into an old cassette machine and pressed play. Connors' message to Adrian's answering machine came on.

'Who's that?' Lucy asked.

'I don't know. I was hoping you might recognise it.'

135

She shook her head. 'Where does it come from? How long have you had it?'

'It was a message left on Adrian's answerphone, the phone you gave to me, remember? I reckon that was what the people who ransacked my hotel room were looking for.'

'You should have it locked away somewhere safe, it could be—'

'This is a copy,' Jed interrupted. 'The master is with Detective Inspector McClusky at the Met.'

'Oh, well, that's all right then.' She paused. 'Isn't it?'

'Well . . . yeah.' He looked confused. 'Isn't it?'

'Oh!' Lucy summed up both their feelings of frustration, confusion, sadness and fear. 'I don't know.' Jed clasped her hand and they looked intently at one another.

Quimby had arranged to meet Archie on a bridge outside Newcastle. His headlights cut through the fog as he parked and walked to the mid-point of the bridge. There was no one there. He padded around for a few minutes wondering if he had been set up, then Archie appeared out of the shadows.

'Filthy night,' Quimby said, conversationally.

'Have you got the money?' Archie asked, ignoring the attempt at geniality.

Quimby handed over a bundle of notes, which Archie started counting. Realising it wasn't all there, he looked questioningly at Quimby. 'Half now,' the reporter explained, 'the rest when it goes to press.'

'That's not the agreement.'

'It's the best I can do.'

'All right.' Archie appeared to give in. 'What do you want to know?'

Quimby's hands were shaking with excitement as he pulled out a contract letter and his tape machine. His excitement gave way to fear as more shapes appeared in the darkness and those he recognised as Big Chrissie, Omo and Bobby closed in round him. 'What's going on?' he squeaked.

'It's like this,' Archie explained, 'we've had our little chat. I'm keeping your money and you are gonna go home to London, and never show your face up here again.'

'Piss off.' Quimby's anger managed to conquer his fear. 'Who do you think you are, eh? You're nothing but a bunch of Northern dole boys. I'll have the law all over you.'

'Somehow I doubt that,' Archie said as Big Chrissie reached into the plastic bag he was carrying and pulled out an impossibly large vibrator.

'Bloody hell!' Quimby's fears overtook his bravado again. 'What are you going to do with that?'

Big Chrissie smiled. 'I'm not going to be doing anything with it.'

Quimby's eyes widened as he realised what they intended. 'Oh, no,' he moaned, 'no!'

'You should think yourself lucky.' Big Chrissie seemed slightly offended. 'This is our number-one best seller.'

Omo pulled out a camcorder and Big Chrissie emptied a selection of painful looking sexual aids onto the ground from his bag.

'My photographer's over there.' Quimby pointed into the fog. 'He'll be shooting all this, I'm warning you.'

'Nice night for it,' Bobby said, and grinned widely.

'All right.' Quimby's mind was racing. 'Forget it. I'll walk away. I'll just take my money and I'll walk away.'

'What money?' Archie asked.

'I've got to have something to write about,' Quimby whined. 'How can I explain away the dosh?'

'Write about anything you like, bonny lad,' Archie advised him, 'but not about us, or Jed. Or else this little film will come back to haunt you.'

'What little film?'

'The one we're about to make,' Archie said as Omo moved in with the camera. Big Chrissie took the vibrator in one hand and a pot of lubricating jelly in the other – and Quimby fainted away.

The following day Pep was waving a tabloid newspaper at Emma. A bold headline shouted: FROM BANK CLERK TO LOAN SHARK – THE NORTH-EAST'S MODERN-DAY SHYLOCK.

'I don't know anything about it,' Emma pleaded.

'Then how in hell did they get all this detail? You lying, deceitful bitch!' He cuffed her across the face.

'Please, Pep . . .'

'Please, Pep? You should have thought about that before you had your little natter to the press.' He cuffed her again. Outside the room

138

Beckie began to cry. Pep turned and shouted at the child, 'Are you gonna be quiet?' Emma came up behind him, in a daze, with a hammer in her hand. She raised it up and aimed at the back of his skull just as he turned back. 'What the . . .?' He raised his arm and deflected the blow as it fell. His initial shock then turned to a black rage as he advanced on her, holding his arm.

'Oh God . . .' Emma murmured, dropping the hammer, realising that her chance had passed.

Jed and Lucy's lovemaking was reaching a noisy crescendo in the cottage bedroom and they didn't hear the front door open, or the approaching footsteps. Just as Jed was about to climax the bedroom door swung open and Wendy stood on the threshold, gazing open-mouthed at the scene.

'Oh God!' Jed couldn't think of anything better to say, 'Wendy!'

'Your sister's in hospital, Jed,' Wendy said after what seemed like an age. 'I thought you'd want to know.'

CHAPTER FOURTEEN

Pep was sitting beside Emma's hospital bed, looking guilty. Emma's face was puffed up and swollen, but she still managed to sound kindly as she spoke through bruised lips. 'Do you not think,' she asked cautiously, 'you should maybe . . . talk to somebody about it?'

'About what?' Pep's head came up indignantly.

'About your tempers. Your rages. I'd go with you if you wanted.'

Suddenly he was angry again. 'What, a bloody. . .' He searched for the word, found it and spat it out. 'A bloody therapist?' He saw the fear in her eyes and, remembering where he was, calmed himself down. 'I lost me temper, Emm. I'm really sorry. It'll not happen again.'

'It keeps on happening, though, Pep,' she reasoned, 'time after time after time. Doesn't it?'

'It hasn't been easy of late.' He regained his look of contrition. 'The business has been up and down, mostly down, and then I nearly lost it all with your Jed buggering off on bail. And then there's the wedding . . . it's quite a stressful time, love.'

'I know, Pep, but you can't take it out on me. That's just not fair.'

'Look, Emma, I swear on the lives of my children that nothing like this'll ever happen again. Things'll be fine when we're married. That's what we need.'

'Are you sure about that, Pep?' She wanted so much to believe him.

'Absolutely, love.' He kissed her gently. 'I've just got to learn to lighten up, not take things so seriously, so . . . personally.' This was as near to begging for forgiveness as Pep was ever likely to get and Emma mustered a painful smile, clasping his hand and wrapping her finger round his. 'Mind,' he laughed, relieved to feel he had won her over, 'it was you that started it, with that clout over the nut.' He realised his words weren't funny the moment they came out of his mouth. Pep was used to hearing his jokes die a death.

'Did you offer Jed that job like I asked you?'

'Aye, I did pet.' Jed gratefully grasped at this straw of possible redemption.

'And what did he say?'

'He said okay. I don't think he has much choice at the moment. I think he's pretty strapped.'

Outside the room, Nigel, who was standing guard, saw Jed coming and stepped forward. 'Hang on, Jed,' he warned.

'Button it, pal,' Jed snapped and Nigel decided it was safer not to interfere.

Pep stood up as Jed came in. 'Hello Jed,' he said.

The moment Jed saw the state of Emma's face, he felt rage boil inside him. Almost instinctively he leaped at Pep, grabbing his throat and squeezing with all his strength. The impact of his rush sent them both crashing to the floor where they rolled over and over as Pep thrashed around as if for his very life. Emma screamed, bringing the nurses and Nigel running in. Nigel tried to get a grip on Jed but the fighters were moving too fast, sending bedpans and bottles flying. A side cabinet came down, drenching them in Robinson's Barley Water and Lucozade. Pep's face was starting to turn blue but Jed only tightened his grip, he wanted to kill him.

'Stop it!' Emma shrieked, bringing them both to a halt with Jed's hands still round Pep's windpipe. 'For God's sake,' she said quietly, 'just stop.'

A young woman doctor leaned over and gently tried to ease Jed's fingers open. The look Jed gave her made her step back. 'Just doing my job,' she said, nervously, 'saving lives and all that.'

Jed finally released his grip and Pep took a huge gasp of air. 'Thank you, Doctor,' he managed to say as Nigel helped him to his feet.

'Your time,' Jed snapped, 'would be better spent on someone who was *worth* keeping alive.'

Safely protected by Nigel, Pep was about to say something but thought better of it and kissed Emma goodbye instead, then stared at Jed, daring him to react. Jed said nothing. 'Get well soon, pet,' Pep said and left with Nigel and the doctor.

'One more stunt like that, Mr Peploe,' the doctor warned him once they were outside the room, 'and I'll ring someone and have you removed from the hospital, all right?'

Pep stared at her for a moment before shaking his head. 'That's not how it works, pet,' he said. 'I'm paying for that room, and all the other shit that goes with it, and unless you button your lip, I'll ring someone and have you removed from the hospital.' For a second the doctor seemed to be considering slapping his face but apparently thought better of it, and walked away instead.

In the room, Jed sat down on the edge of his sister's bed. 'I'm amazed he has the cheek to be here,' he said.

'He was trying to say sorry,' Emma said, trying to lighten the atmosphere.

'And that makes all this all right then, does it?'

'It's as much my fault as his. He's been under a lot of pressure and I didn't see it. And I did try to brain him with the hammer.' Jed shook his head, not willing to be convinced. 'Look, Jed, he's sworn on his kids' lives it won't ever happen again. He's promised me he'll work at it.'

'I've seen how he works at it, Emm, and I don't like it.'

'He's under pressure, Jed. You of all people should understand that. You know what it's like, what it does to you.'

'Don't draw parallels between me and Pep. I'm not like him, and I don't like him, and when I get him outside of here—'

'You'll do nothing!' Emma interrupted firmly.

She felt near to tears. 'I don't want any more fighting. I just want to get better, go home, get married and get some bloody sleep!'

Jed's jaw dropped. 'You're never still going to *marry* him?'

'Yes I am, and if you really want to help your little sister, you'll forget all this ever happened, forget and forgive.'

'You've got that the wrong way round.'

'Does it matter?'

'Not really, Emm, 'cause I can't do either.'

'Jed, I'm going to marry Pep. Don't make me choose between you and him.'

He took her hand. 'All right, Emm, if that's what you want.' He kissed her forehead as she smiled and closed her eyes.

Pep was waiting for him outside the hospital with Nigel and Curtis. Jed tensed himself for a fight as Pep made towards him from his car. 'Do you want a lift?' Pep asked.

'You know what it is, Pep?' Jed fought to keep control of himself. 'If I had to choose between sharing a car with you and having my arms cut off, I'd go for the amputation.'

Pep stared at him for a moment. 'Is that any way for a bloke to talk to his boss?'

'I'm working for you, Pep, but don't get all confused, you're not my boss. You'll never be my boss.'

'You owe me, Jed,' Pep reminded him. 'The bail bond business. Don't forget.'

'I owe you nothing after that.' Jed gestured back towards Emma's room.

'I'll see you tomorrow then,' Pep taunted him. 'Don't be late.'

Jed watched them drive off before walking to the bus stop.

As Warren Bowles stepped out of his private jet at Elstree Aerodrome, he was surprised to find Lucy waiting beside his Mercedes on the tarmac. 'Lucy,' he beamed, 'it's always a pleasure to see you, but what on earth could be so urgent?'

'It's Jed,' she said.

'Now what's he done?' Bowles sighed.

'It's not what *he's* done,' she said, climbing into the car ahead of him. 'We've been sifting through all the paperwork relating to First Ade Management's finances.'

'Sifting?' Bowles was still smiling as the car pulled smoothly away. 'That sounds like fun.'

'I wish. It turns out everything Adrian gave me, Jed paid for, but didn't know it. My car, my apartment, holidays . . .'

'I don't believe it, Adrian? Your brother was a lot of things, Lucy, but—'

Lucy held up the envelope she was carrying. 'It's all in here. You can't argue with bank statements. I'm so embarrassed.'

'Looks like Jed almost owns you.' Bowles gazed into her eyes, wanting her desperately. 'Now that's an asset worth having.'

'Please, Warren.' Lucy's mind was on other things.

'Why don't you let me reimburse Jed, on your

behalf?' Bowles asked after a few moments'
thought.

'What, so then you would own me?' She shook
her head. 'Thank you for the offer, but it wouldn't
solve anything. I need to find out why my brother
died. I thought I'd talk to Alan Clarke, see if he
could shed any light on just how Adrian siphoned
off Jed's money. And just how much. What do you
think?'

Bowles became lost in thought for a few
moments. 'It's a good idea,' he said eventually,
'but I think I may have an even better one. How's
about I organize a meet with the record company's
head of business affairs? That way there can be no
bullshit.'

'Do you think you could do that?'

'Of course I could. That is, unless you think Jed
would prefer to—'

Lucy shook her head. 'Jed's scared to do anything. Seems like every time he moves someone
ends up dead.'

Bowles put his arm round her and hugged.
'There's nothing to worry about. One way or
another, I'll take care of it. What are you going to
do with those?' He nodded towards the envelope.

'Give them to the police?'

'McClusky?' he asked. 'Good idea.'

Pep and Beckie were alone together in the house
that night. Pep did his best to make them both
some tea and laid it out in the dining room. Beckie
sat at the far end of the table and stared at him,
ignoring the plate in front of her.

'I hate you,' she said.

Pep nodded, embarrassed. He couldn't blame her for feeling that way. 'Eat your dinner, pet,' he said as kindly as he could. But Beckie just kept staring. 'Listen, Beckie. We're going up to see your mam tomorrow. She'll get all worried if she thinks you're not eating your meals.' She kept staring. 'Please?' She picked up her fork and poked at the food. 'Thank you.'

That night in the Legion Club, Pep was the topic of conversation. 'Swore on his kids' lives, eh?' Archie muttered. 'Not on his own? Typical of the little shit. What did you say?'

'What *can* you say?' Jed wanted to know.

'You don't say anything to people like that,' Big Chrissie suggested. 'You chin them.'

'I tried that,' Jed admitted.

'And you're still going to work for him?' Omo asked.

'It's a way of keeping an eye on the little twat. Make sure he doesn't start with Emma again. And it's a job.' Jed shrugged. 'I need the money.'

'Ah, now,' Omo said, taking his cue, 'we've been thinking about that, your predicament. We had an idea.'

'I've told you before,' Jed said, 'I'm not modelling for your catalogue.'

'No, seriously,' Omo persisted, 'there's a new community centre opening for underprivileged children. David Laidlaw's kid's gonna go there.'

'It's a council place,' Big Chrissie chipped in,

'but it's had some private-sector bunce put into it, and they want to get a bit of publicity in return for their generosity.'

'That's fair enough,' Archie declared. 'Good cause.'

'Anyway,' Omo continued, 'we thought it would be like a nice gesture for you to do the honours. Cut the ribbon or what have you.'

'Nah,' Jed said, 'not my scene, all that.'

'There's a monkey in it,' Omo said casually.

'Five hundred quid,' Big Chrissie added.

'Cash,' Omo said.

'On the day,' Big Chrissie added.

'In your mitt. You'd be able to tell Pep to bugger off,' Omo continued.

Jed shook his head. 'I have a problem with all that celebrity stuff, you know?'

'Five hundred big ones,' Omo kept going. 'Nee questions asked, for ten minutes' graft.'

'I'll do it!' Archie volunteered.

'There you are,' Jed said, 'Archie'll do it.'

'That's nee good, man,' Omo protested. 'Nee bugger knows who he is.'

'Howway, Jed,' Big Chrissie said, trying a different tack, 'it's for the kids.'

'Oh, please, Chrissie, don't lay that one on me.'

'They'd love it, man.' Omo followed the same tack. 'Jed the pop star coming to see them.'

'I'm not Jed the pop star, not any more. As of now I'm Jed the bloke who works at his brother-in-law's warehouse.'

'Well,' Omo said, 'if you change your mind . . .'

'I won't,' Jed assured him, getting up and heading for the bar.

'We'll see,' Omo murmured, with a sneaky glint in his eye.

CHAPTER FIFTEEN

It was bucketing down with rain on Jed's first day at the warehouse, but he still managed to be early, much to Pep's annoyance. As Jed came in, Pep, his bruised neck hidden by an expensive paisley cravat, was counting some stacked boxes labelled 'seconds - imperfect'.

'Morning,' Jed said.

'See this?' Pep opened one of the boxes and pulled out a bundle of denim, showing him the labels that had been cut in half to show they were seconds. 'We replace the cut ones with these good ones.' He held up an uncut label. 'See?'

'So making seconds into firsts?' Jed suggested.

'You catch on quick.'

'I wish I could say the same about my sister.' Jed waited to see if Pep would take the bait, he wanted an excuse to lay into him, but Pep just smiled. 'You want them all done?'

Pep nodded. 'Unless you've got anything else planned.' He handed Jed the good labels and an industrial stapler before walking off towards his office. Halfway there he stopped, aware of Jed's eyes burning into the back of his head. 'What?'

'Nothing.' Jed bit his lip and started stapling with a vengeance.

'Get the motor, Nigel,' Pep instructed. 'Curtis! Keep an eye on things here while I'm out,' he nodded towards Jed as he stapled steadily away and Curtis chuckled. He got the message.

Emma and Beckie were at the bridal shop, having the finishing touches put to their dresses. As the elderly seamstress made the last alterations and the sales assistant helped Emma into the dress they both noticed the bruise on her side.

'Nasty bruise,' the assistant commented.

'Yeah,' Emma avoided her eyes, 'it was a nasty fall.'

'Must've been.'

'Can we go now, Mam?' Beckie asked.

'Soon, pet,' Emma assured her. 'Can we get on?' she asked the assistant. As the dress was zipped up and Emma turned to the mirror all their worries were forgotten.

'Oh Mam!' Beckie exclaimed. 'You look like a princess.'

On the private estate in Cochrane Park where she lived, Pep spotted her. She was walking towards her house – her house and her new husband. He watched her for a while, then climbed out of the parked car. 'Mary?'

She turned, her face full of dread. 'What?'

'Did you get the invitation?' he asked.

'Yes.'

'If I remember rightly, it had RSVP written at the bottom of it.'

'I was going to reply,' Mary said.

'You're leaving it a bit late, aren't you?'

'Why do you want me to be there, Pep? It's someone else's day.'

Pep shrugged. 'So's we can put all of our stuff behind us.'

'I've already done that.'

Pep was becoming irritated. 'The invitation wasn't just to you, you know. I'd like for the kids to be there.' He tried to sound as sincere as he could. 'I really would.'

Mary shook her head as if trying to clear memories of their past life. 'You're so plausible, aren't you?'

A man's whistle attracted both their attention. Bob, Mary's husband, was standing at the gate of their house. He waved at Mary, checking that everything was all right. She nodded and waved back. Pep waved too but Bob ignored him. 'I'm glad you found somebody else, you know,' Pep said.

'So am I.' She thought for a second. 'I'll talk to the kids. If they want to be there then we'll come.' Pep nodded, knowing that was the best he could hope for, and went back to the car. He watched as Mary returned to Bob, who kissed her at the gate. Then he drove away.

The smirking Curtis was still watching Jed work when the phone rang. 'Hoy,' he shouted across the warehouse, 'call for you.'

Jed came over and took the phone. 'Hello?'

'Jed, it's Lucy.'

'Hello Lucy . . . just a minute.' He looked at Curtis. 'Do you mind?'

Curtis smiled. 'Not at all.' He obviously didn't intend to move and Jed decided it wasn't worth pursuing.

'Sorry, Lucy, go on . . .'

'Warren's managed to arrange a meet with the head of corporate finance at your record company. He should be able to shed some light on things. Think you can make it?'

'When?'

'The day after tomorrow.'

'I'll be there.'

Curtis looked at his watch and tapped its face, staring pointedly at Jed, 'Come on!'

'See you soon,' Jed said into the phone. 'And well done, Lucy.'

'Lucy!' Curtis raised an eyebrow as Jed hung up the phone, making the name sound as sleazy as possible. Jed walked over to him and drew a line in the dust on the floor with his foot.

'See that?' Jed asked.

'Yeah.'

'That's the line. Don't cross it!' As Jed went back to his stapling Curtis stared at the line.

Emma and Pep had come together in the large function room at the Post House Hotel, with the catering manager and a florist. Emma was studying a list while Beckie wandered around the edges of the room, bored.

'Who replaced the champagne with sparkling wine?' Emma asked. The eyes of the catering manager and florist turned to Pep.

'If you look,' he smiled guiltily, 'what I ordered

154

was champagne for the first bottle and then sparkling after that.'

'Why?'

'Well, who's gonna know the difference after the first bottle's gone down?'

'Me.' Emma was obviously determined.

Pep held up his hands in surrender and looked at the catering manager. 'Change it back to champagne, would you please?' The manager nodded, delighted.

'And I thought there were going to be flowers on every table,' Emma went on. All eyes returned to Pep.

'I thought it would have more effect,' he suggested, 'just you having them.' Emma gave him an exasperated look and he raised his eyebrows at the florist, who nodded happily.

'That's fine, then,' Emma said.

'As long as you're happy, my love.'

She gave him a hug. 'I'm thrilled.'

'Not be long now, then,' the florist said, 'until the big day.'

'Eeh, I know,' Emma said, suddenly serious, 'and there's still so much to get done. I'm gonna have to have some help, Pep.' Pep was about to protest but she cut him off. 'No, no, I don't mean you. You've got enough on your plate running the business. I mean with Beckie. I need someone to mind her while I'm out running around.'

'One of the boys can look after her,' Pep suggested. 'I'll sort it.'

'Nigel and Curtis?' Emma looked horrified. 'Minding the bairn? No you bloody won't!'

Pep looked mystified, he didn't seem able to do anything right. 'That's their job,' he protested, 'minding.' He thought for a second. 'All right, maybe not.' He considered it a few seconds longer and then his eyes lit up. 'You just leave it to me.'

Jed was just coming out of the toilets when he saw Pep coming back into the warehouse. 'Where's my future brother-in-law?' Pep wanted to know. 'Got a major job for you tomorrow, Jed. Question is, are you responsible enough to handle it?'

'What is it?'

'Your sister's got lots of running around to do, before she and me tie the knot. So she needs some help, at home.' He grinned. 'Babysitting your niece.'

'Ah,' Curtis laughed, 'isn't that nice?'

'When?' Jed asked.

'Tomorrow. Think you can handle it?'

Jed ignored their mockery. 'I can handle it.'

'What about Lucy?' Curtis teased.

'Lucy?' Pep's eyes widened.

'I said, I can handle it.'

'Right then.' Pep realised he had pushed Jed as far as was safe. 'It's a date. In the meantime, back to the stapling, if you would. If you're running low on jackets, there's another artic-load out in the car park.'

That night Jed plucked up the courage to go out to Wendy's house. He rang the bell and a moment later the intercom buzzed into life. 'What do you want, Jed?'

'I've got the keys to your uncle's cottage.'

The intercom went dead and Wendy opened the door. Jed handed her the keys. 'You and Lucy finished with it, then, have you? You should've just posted them on.'

'I thought about it,' he admitted, 'but I wanted to talk to you.'

'I'd like the keys to this place back as well.' He gave them back to her and she looked directly at him. 'Don't you want to sleep with me, Jed?'

'I, er . . .' He couldn't muster his thoughts in time.

'I mean, I've been trying to get you into bed since you came out of prison. But no, there's always been some excuse. You wanted your own space. I gave you your own space. You needed to get your head together somewhere. I gave you the keys to my cottage. And what do you go and do there?'

'It was complicated, Wendy,' he protested. 'I mean, you have to bear in mind that Lucy's recently bereaved—'

'Oh,' Wendy jumped in, 'so it was a sympathy shag, was it?'

'No, it . . . I'd just found out I'd bought her a car you see, and a house . . .' Wendy's eyes grew wider with every word he said. 'And I was just trying to make her feel better . . .'

'Well, it certainly sounded like you were doing that!'

'But I don't feel the same way about you.'

'You don't?' Wendy was so angry she looked as if she might hit him, but she slammed the door in his face instead.

Jed knew he had said the wrong thing again. 'I love you,' he murmured. 'I just wish I could tell you that.' The light in the hallway went out as he turned his collar up and walked off into the cold night.

Babysitting Beckie the next day was a relief after working in the warehouse. Jed was busily pushing her on the swing in Pep's garden when Omo and Big Chrissie appeared round the side of the house.

'How, Jed?' Omo greeted him.

'What are you two doing around here?' Jed asked. 'Don't tell me people's stopped dying?'

'One last plea,' Big Chrissie said, 'from the heart.'

'I've said no.' Jed was firm.

'Believe it or not,' Omo persevered, 'these kids are really big fans of yours! It would mean the world to them. If you don't turn up they're gonna be stuck with the bloody Lord Mayor, and everyone hates him.'

'Why would anyone want to be the Lord Mayor, anyway?' Chrissie wondered.

'You get to wear one of them nice gold chokers round your neck,' Omo suggested.

'There's that, like,' Chrissie agreed.

'Look, lads,' Jed said, interrupting their double act, 'I told you, I just want a quiet life. I've done that meet-and-greet business a few times and it's just not my bag, you know? I find the whole thing . . .' Words failed him.

'I know you're dead set against it,' Omo jumped back in, 'but I thought, well I mean . . . I know you could do with the money.'

'Why won't you help the children, Uncle Jed?' Beckie chirped up.

'It's a long story, pet,' Jed told her and then turned angrily on Omo. 'Now see what you've started?'

'I like long stories,' Beckie said.

'You're gonna leave a lot of little bairns disappointed,' Omo warned him.

'Bairns like Beckie,' Chrissie added, 'only not so lucky.'

Jed said nothing. They walked off shaking their heads, leaving him to his guilt and angst.

Once they were out of earshot, Omo asked, 'Think he'll go for it?'

'After that?' Chrissie nodded confidently. 'He'll never be able to live with the guilt!'

Jed and Beckie were hand in hand, walking in the park. A group of lads were playing football on the grass. One of them spotted him and started singing 'Crocodile Shoes'.

That was all he needed. Parks were for peace and quiet, weren't they?

'Is this the cowboy dream, is it, Jed?' One of them shouted. 'Takin' your sprog to the park?'

He tried to avoid eye contact.

'Ride 'em, cowboy,' another youth jeered. 'Yippee ay-o!'

'"Cowboy dreams . . ."' a third sang mockingly. 'Stupid daft twat!'

Jed continued to ignore them and walked Beckie over to the playground, where she ran off to the sandpit while Jed sank onto a bench. A group of mothers, watching their children, started nudging one another and whispering. Eventually one of them, a pretty woman, came over. 'You're Jed Shepperd, aren't you?' she enquired.

'I look like him,' Jed shook his head, 'so I'm told.'

'He says he's not,' she called back to her friends.

'That *is* him,' another shouted back. 'I've got his record at home, with his picture on it.'

'Do you want to come and sit with us over here?' the woman asked him.

'I'm happy where I am.' He smiled. 'Thank you very much.'

'It's not often we get a pop star at the swings,' another mother piped up.

'I've told you,' Jed insisted, 'I'm not who you think I am.'

'You look like him,' the first woman said. 'So it doesn't really matter if you're him or not, does it?'

Jed shook his head again, declining her obvious invitation. 'I'm having half an hour with my niece.'

'Your niece?' The second woman came over to join them. 'She's not your daughter, then?'

'No.' Jed remained patient. 'She's my niece.'

'You're not married then?'

'Er . . .' Jed tried to think of the best answer.

'So would you like to spend the morning with some bored young mums?' They all looked at Jed and he realised they were serious. He stood up quickly.

'Beckie,' he called, 'time to go, love.'

'Oh,' Becky was disappointed, 'Uncle Jed, man.'

The first mother pounced. 'She called you Jed!' You *are* him!'

'You lied to us,' her friend said bitterly, 'and I bought your record!'

'We've got to get going.' He was beginning to panic and shouted, 'Beckie!'

'It's people like us what makes people like you, you know,' one of the women said, 'puts you where you are.'

As Beckie came over Jed gripped her hand firmly. 'I don't wish to seem ungrateful,' he told them, 'but I honestly wish you hadn't bothered.' As he walked off he could hear them grumbling to one another and vowing never to buy any more of his records. The lads started up their taunts again as he approached, turning 'Crocodile Shoes' into a football chant. Beckie had to run to keep up with her uncle's long strides as he hurried to escape the sounds of their voices.

When Jed and Beckie got back to the warehouse he could see Emma and Pep inside the office. It looked as if Pep was about to start wagging his finger when he spotted them through the glass

and backed off. Emma came out and swept Beckie
up in her arms.

'Hiya, have you had a good day?'

'Great!' Jed said.

'I'd better get you home for your tea, eh?' Emma
said. 'No doubt you'll be starving.'

'Uncle Jed bought me lots of sweets and
chocolate.'

'Well,' Emma said, 'uncles are allowed to do
that' – she glanced at Jed – 'once in a while.
Got to go,' she said to Pep. 'See you later.' She
kissed him and headed for the door, still cuddling
Beckie.

As Emma went out Jed turned and saw Pep
looking him up and down. 'What?' Jed asked.

Pep shook his head. 'I'm just looking at you.
What I see makes me sad.'

'Don't let it make you sad,' Jed said, keeping a
tight lid on his temper.

'Oh, but it does, Jed. You've come home with
your tail between your legs, and not so much as
a pot to piss in. So I give you a job and now here
you are, stapling labels into cheap, tatty jackets.
Look at yourself, man, what do you see? Loser.
Loser with a great big L.'

'You think I'm a loser, Pep?'

'What is there to make me think otherwise?'
Pep laughed, glancing at Curtis. 'Tell us, please.'

'All right, I'll tell you. I tasted it, Pep. I lived
the dream. Maybe only for a little minute, but I
was there, breathed that rarefied air and even if
I never get back there, even if I have to live in
the gutter next to dirt like you, I've done it, Pep.

I've been somewhere you'll never visit. And in my book, pal, that makes me a winner.'

Pep, unable to think of an answer, turned angrily and walked off, while Curtis headed into the toilets. Jed waited a moment and then followed Curtis.

He found him doing his hair in the mirror.

'Curtis?'

'Yeah?' Curtis turned and Jed smacked him on the chin, sending him to the floor, dazed. Jed knelt down beside him.

'I have to take that shit from Pep,' he said, 'but not from the likes of you.' He stood up and walked out with a pleasant, 'See you!'

'Found any rarities lately?' Jed asked Wendy brightly as they sat that evening in a bistro.

He had managed to persuade her to come out for dinner. She'd agreed, but seemed determined not to make it easy for him.

'Oh, you know, the odd' – she looked at him tellingly – 'surprise.'

'If you're trying to make me feel guilty, Wendy, then it's working.'

'What did you expect? A plate of food and a glass of wine and all is forgiven?' She took a drink.

'How's the wine?' he asked.

'Fine,' she replied, grudgingly.

'Thank Christ for that! Listen, you know my sister's getting married on the nineteenth of this month. Well, I was wondering if you fancied—'

'Making it a double wedding? No thanks.'

'. . . If you fancied coming along. With me.'

'Lucy busy that day, is she?'

'I don't know,' he sighed. 'The thing is . . . I'm gonna play, at the reception, just a couple of songs with the house band. But one's a song of mine, and it's new, and . . . well, I'd like you to be there.'

Wendy hid her surprise and keenness. 'All right. But I don't want to talk about it tonight. Call me tomorrow.'

'Er, tomorrow?'

'Is that a problem?'

'Not a problem, as such. It's just that I'll not be here. I've got, er . . . to go to London. I've got a . . . business meeting.'

'With who?' Wendy was suspicious.

'Oh . . .' Jed played for time. 'Various people, you know, record company, publishers . . .'

'Lucy?'

'Lucy? Er . . . yes.'

Wendy threw down her fork with a clatter and shouted, making heads turn in their direction. 'I don't believe this.'

'She arranged the meeting, Wendy.' Jed was fighting for his life. 'She arranged for my ticket and everything.'

'Everything?' She got to her feet and he grabbed her arm.

'Wendy, wait a minute, please.' She sat down again reluctantly. 'There's a lot of money missing, my money, and there are people dead! Now, I'm going to London to see if I can get it all sorted. I have to. Yes?' At that moment the waiter arrived with their main courses. 'What's this?' Jed asked.

'Vermicelli,' the waiter informed him.

'I ordered ratatouille,' Jed said.

'Never mind.' Wendy stopped the waiter as he went to remove the plates. 'I'm not hungry any more.' With that she got up and walked out. Jed hung his head and sighed deeply.

CHAPTER SIXTEEN

Dick Pilsbury's office was designed to make him appear impressive behind his massive desk, but Warren Bowles gave no indication of being intimidated as he sat with Lucy and Jed on the other side.

'This seems to me to be a very shoddy way to treat a major-league artist, Mr Pilsbury,' he said.

'Please,' Pilsbury interrupted him, 'call me Dick.'

'Not yet,' Bowles snapped, bringing a faint smile to Jed's lips as Pilsbury bristled visibly. 'Our information suggests that Paradigm Records haven't been as straight with Mr Shepperd as they might've been.' Both Jed and Lucy were startled and impressed by his directness.

'I'm sure,' Pilsbury said, trying to calm him, 'you appreciate that a company like Paradigm expects, indeed depends upon, some kind of a return on its investment. We ploughed a lot of money into Jed. All we got in return was a lot of excuses from Mr Shepperd's late manager. Subsequently, Jed as a commodity . . .' He paused and nodded to Jed. 'Sorry Jed,' he said, then, turning back to Bowles, continued: 'Jed as a commodity became, in the opinion of our shareholders, a moral and financial liability. We have nothing to hide, Mr Bowles.'

'Then you won't object to an audit?'

Pilsbury seemed to pale, but kept going. 'You're contractually entitled, given reasonable notice, to audit this company's accounts, at your expense. We have no objection to that.'

'Then we'll be looking to do just that,' Bowles assured him. 'My accountant will be in touch.' He stood up to demonstrate that the meeting was over. 'Thank you for your time, Dick.'

'If I can be of any more help, please let me know.'

As they made their way to the door Bowles paused. 'I'm just gonna write down the details of my accountants,' he said. 'Won't be a moment.' Lucy and Jed went out ahead of him.

'You're sailing a bit close to the wind, aren't you?' Pilsbury said once they were alone.

'I thought it went rather well,' Bowles grinned. 'Thoroughly convinced me, you did.'

'We've only put off the inevitable. Six months or a year from now and you're still looking at the same net result. If you audit—'

'Audits cost money and Jed's broke,' Bowles cut in. 'My accountants will tell him whatever I want him to hear.'

Outside the office Jed and Lucy were slightly shell-shocked. 'He takes no prisoners, eh?' Lucy said.

'Warren? I'd rather have him as a friend than an enemy, that's for sure,' Jed agreed. 'But how am I going to pay for audits and accountants? I can't even pay for my own train ticket!'

'Let's wait and see what Warren has to say, eh?' Lucy suggested. 'I didn't like Pilsbury. What a shit.'

'We should talk to Alan Clarke,' Jed said. 'At least find out why he left.'

'Would you like me to do it?'

'I've got to get back up the road.'

'It's a full-fare ticket,' she reminded him. 'If you want to stay the night . . .' She let the suggestion hang temptingly in the air.

For a second Jed considered setting her straight about his feelings for Wendy, but he chickened out. 'I've got to be up there for a stag night,' he said lamely. 'My sister's getting married.'

'Oh.' Lucy turned cool. 'Right.'

'Plus, I'm playing at my sister's wedding and—'

'You're playing again?' She brightened up. 'Great!'

'Yeah, just one song, but I'm kind of nervous. It's been a while. I want to get back and just make sure I'm on top of things.'

'You're good when you're on top of things, Jed,' she teased, making him swallow hard. 'I enjoyed my little trip to Holy Island.'

'I have to go.'

'Always running, Jed. Can't keep it up forever, you know.' He nodded and then shook his head and left. 'Have a good stag night.'

No one was having a better time at the stag night than Pep himself. Jed, Archie, Omo and Big Chrissie watched as he mooched around

169

the pub dance floor with two young women, a buttock in each hand. The song on the jukebox was Jed's 'Cowboy Dreams'. 'I knew paying your bail money would come in useful one day, Jed!' he shouted across, winking and squeezing the girls' buttocks in time to the music while he told them how he had rescued Jed from a fate worse than death.

'I'm truly tempted,' Archie muttered.

'To do what?' Jed asked.

'To go over there and smack him in the mouth.'

'My brother-in-law-to-be?' Jed exclaimed with mock horror. 'I can't let you do that! Wouldn't do any good.'

'Who says?' asked Archie. 'Your modern-men's magazines?'

'Well,' Jed said, thinking about it, 'just save it until after the wedding photos, would you?'

Omo leaned forward, putting his mouth close to Jed's ear. 'Charity.'

'What?'

'You could give your fee to charity.'

'If you don't want the money,' Chrissie explained, 'there's plenty of others that would be happy to take it.'

'And be glad of it,' Omo agreed.

'Can you two not get it through your heads?' Jed said. 'I'm not doing it! And that's final.'

'Not doing what?' Archie joined in.

'They want Jed to open the new community centre,' Omo reminded him. 'You know, where the old Warrior Street School used to be?'

'Oh, aye.' Archie's eyes misted over at the

memories. 'I used to go there, when I was little, Warrior Street.' He gave Jed a stern look. 'You've got to do that, man.'

'Oh,' Jed exclaimed, 'don't you start!'

'No,' Archie persisted, 'you've got to. Put something back, even if you've messed up big-time yourself, like what you have, you've got to try and encourage them bairns.'

'Absolutely,' Chrissie agreed.

'That's what we've been telling him,' Omo added.

'Me old school.' Archie smiled fondly.

'All right!' Jed gave in. 'All right, you win. I'll do it.'

'Yay!' Omo whooped. 'Good lad.'

'On the condition . . .'

'What?' Omo and Chrissie asked in unison.

'That my fee's given back to the centre.'

They both stared at him in amazement for a second and then Chrissie embraced him, swinging him round. 'What a man!' At that moment Jed saw Pep disappearing into the ladies' with one of the girls from the dance floor. Jed tried to break free of Chrissie's grip to go after them but the big man wouldn't release him. 'Let it go, Jed,' he said. 'It's his stag night.'

Jed thought for a second and then nodded his agreement. Chrissie let him go. 'I'll see you tomorrow,' Jed said, making for the door.

'You certainly will, mate,' Omo assured him. He seemed hardly able to believe that they had actually managed to talk him into doing the opening at the last moment. As Jed made his

way out a drunken woman launched herself at
him in search of an autograph.

Chrissie and Omo drifted off in search of the
fruit machine.

'If the opening's at eleven,' Chrissie said, 'and
the wedding's at twelve, it's going to be tight.'

'It's got to be done,' Omo reminded him, 'for
the kiddies!' At that moment the bells on the fruit
machine started to whoop and money cascaded
into the payout trough. 'Jackpot!' Omo cried.

'Well I never,' Big Chrissie said, holding up
the large magnet he had been using to manipu-
late the fruits. They scooped up their winnings,
and as they turned from the machine they saw
Pep emerge from the ladies' followed by one of
the women whose arses he'd been fondling – a
blonde. His face wore a huge smirk.

Jed grabbed a cab outside the pub and headed for
Pep's house. A little unsteady on his feet, he managed to make it to the door and leaned on the bell.

Emma opened the door. 'Hello,' she said. She
seemed surprised to see him. 'I thought you'd be
out with Pep.'

'I was,' Jed slurred. 'I have been, but I wanted
to see you.'

They went through to the dining room and
Emma found them a bottle of wine to share. 'Not
long to go now, then,' Jed said, 'until you're Mrs
Peploe.'

Emma glanced at the clock, which told her it
was a quarter past midnight. 'By rights I should
be getting some sleep, but I'm too excited.'

'Lot to be excited about, I suppose.'

'Yes.'

'You don't sound too convinced.'

'I'll get there,' she assured him.

'You'll get there? Is that the right way to go into this? I mean it's supposed to be about love and passion and commitment.'

'At my age, Jed, and in my situation, it's also about compromise. It's different for you: you've never compromised, on anything, and I admire that. But I have to think about Beckie. I want to give her a life. I mean a real life. And I want some company myself.'

'Marriage shouldn't just be about companionship, Emm,' he pleaded. 'You should hold out for the whole lot, for love.'

'Pep's the right man for me right now in my life,' she said firmly, 'and I'm glad of him. You didn't see them queuing up outside the door when you came in, did you?'

'You sure you're doing the right thing?'

'No. But it's a chance and I'm gonna take it, like you did.'

'Christ,' Jed said suddenly, looking very depressed, 'don't use me as an example!'

'How are things between you and Wendy?' Emma asked brightly.

'Fine.'

'How are things between you and Lucy?'

'Fine.'

'How are things between you and Wendy and Lucy?' Jed closed his eyes, trying to block out the thoughts. 'You can't keep that up, you know.'

'I know.'

'It's wrong.'

'I know!'

'It's not fair on anyone.'

'I'm not here to talk about my headaches, Emma,' he insisted. 'You're getting married in the morning.'

'Ding dong the bells are gonna chime,' she joked.

'To Pep! I mean, he's . . . he's—'

'Jed.' She cut him off in mid-sentence. 'I really want this marriage to work, and I want us all to get along. Now, I know you mean well, but you coming round here slagging Pep off isn't helping.'

Jed sat quietly for a moment. 'Do you love him, Emm?' he asked eventually.

She thought for a moment. 'I've got to get some sleep.'

'Do you?'

'Jed!' She was becoming angry. 'I'm tired.'

He got up and made for the door, glancing at a shelf loaded down with bottles. 'Can I take one of these?'

'As long as you can walk tomorrow. You're giving me away, remember? And you've promised to sing me a song.' Jed, wincing at the reminder, helped himself to a bottle of vodka and gave his sister a big hug.

A few hours later he was walking along the edge of the surf with half the bottle inside him, talking to a passing seagull. 'You've seen a lot of the world. From up there. You've been around a lot. What do you think I should do?'

The gull didn't answer so Jed went on. 'I mean, should I be telling her about Pep, tonight, off into the toilet with some bird? Should I tell her that men like that don't change? Can't change? Maybe I should just chin him, knock him out, so's he doesn't make it to the wedding in the morning.' He chuckled at the thought. 'Or kidnap Emma and take her far away. To Holy Island, or somewhere. Should I just tell her what I saw? What I know?'

The gull watched him beadily. 'On the other hand, of course, who am I to talk? I mean, who am I to get in the way of what little bit of happiness Emma might be able to carve for herself and her bairn? What should I do? What would you do?'

The gull still didn't reply so Jed took another swig from the bottle. 'Ah, what do you know? I'll tell you what you know, you know nowt! I need to talk to somebody with more sense.'

He walked off and was struck by another thought. 'You and Pep's a lot alike, you know,' he told the bird. 'He says nowt and goes around shitting on people too.'

CHAPTER SEVENTEEN

O mo and Chrissie found Jed the next morning lying fully clothed and face down on Archie's carpet, the empty bottle of vodka still in his hand. As they tried to raise him Archie staggered past them.

'We're late,' Chrissie said.

'What for?' Jed began to come round.

'Be a miracle if he can open his eyes,' Archie commented, 'never mind a community centre. See you at the wedding.' He padded off back to bed.

Omo and Chrissie hauled Jed to his feet and dragged him to the door, grabbing his tux and white shirt as they went. 'Think he'll be all right?' Omo asked.

'He's only got to cut a ribbon,' Chrissie said.

'For the wedding, I meant.'

'Oh.' Chrissie shrugged. It didn't look too hopeful.

Outside the house they bundled him into the waiting minicab, changing him into his wedding clothes as the car sped off.

The community centre wasn't quite finished but the local dignitaries were posing in front of it anyway for the photographers, local TV news crews and building workers. A group of children, brought in for the occasion, were being ignored by everyone as the Lord Mayor made his speech.

'It is with no small dollop of pride that I stand here before you this morning. This community centre not only symbolises the care and concern of the city council, but it also symbolises the part that can be played by private investment in its support of such care.'

There were a few disgruntled mumblings in the crowd and one voice rang out, 'Tight bastard!'

'No, no,' the Lord Mayor insisted, 'private sponsorship can work, and this city council for one will continue to support it. And here before you is the net result.'

As he prattled on Jed's taxi drew up and the press made a rush for it, much to the annoyance of the Lord Mayor, and even more to the annoyance of his wife who had been happily preening herself in the reflected limelight.

Omo and Big Chrissie, doing a good impression of minders, steered the unsteady star to the podium and the crowd gave a cheer, which the Lord Mayor acknowledged graciously. The project manager then took over the microphone.

'Hello. I'll keep this short and sweet. I must thank Neptune Industries for supporting the centre, and all the people that worked so hard, for so little, to build the thing. I'd also like to thank our own local hero, Jed Shepperd' (Jed received another cheer) 'for interrupting what I

know is a very busy schedule, to come here and
do the honours. Good to see a local lad flying the
flag, Jed.' Jed waved down the cheering crowd but
didn't move. 'Jed?' The project manager tried to
cue him again.

Getting the hint, Jed lurched up onto the
podium and approached the microphone. 'I, er,
declare this centre . . . open.'

To more cheers, he was ferried across to a
corner of the new building to pull a drawstring
which unveiled a plaque. He smiled uncomfortably for the cameras, waving in response to the
ever-increasing cheers.

'I'd just like to thank you on a personal note,
Jed,' the project manager said quietly. 'It was
really generous of you to give some of your fee
back to the centre, back to the kiddies.'

It took a second for his meaning to sink in.
'*Some* of my fee, did you say?'

'The five hundred,' the project manager reminded him. 'It's really appreciated, I can tell
you.'

'What was my total fee again?' Jed enquired.

The project manager looked confused. 'Two
thousand. That's right, isn't it? As agreed with
your representatives.'

Jed turned and glowered at Chrissie, who had
his hand over his eyes, and Omo, who offered up
a timid smile. Jed was then led back to the mayor
and his wife and offered champagne, which he
refused with a shudder.

'Would you sign this for me, Jed?' the Lord
Mayor's wife asked, holding up her napkin.

'Sure.' Jed obliged, blearily trying to focus his eyes.

'It's not for me. It's for my niece. She's retarded.'

For a second Jed thought about nutting her, but decided it would hurt too much and smiled instead. 'That would figure.' He looked at his watch. 'Well, if you'll excuse me, I've got to go and give someone away.' He nodded towards the cab and Omo and Chrissie led the way.

'I'm surprised you're travelling around in that thing, mind,' the Lady Mayoress said. 'I thought you'd have a limousine.'

'What's the difference?' Jed shrugged.

'The difference is that anyone can have one of those.'

Jed peered into the cavernous interior of the Lord Mayor's black Daimler limousine. 'Yeah. Whereas it takes a particular type of twat to sit in the back of one of these things, eh?'

'That,' she fumed as he climbed into his cab, 'is the last time I buy one of his records!'

Omo and Big Chrissie knew they had a lot of explaining to do as the car crawled through endless traffic. 'Things have been tight, Jed,' Chrissie said, 'on the mail-order front, and at the cemetery.' He dug Omo in the ribs in search of support.

'Eh?' Omo jerked up in his seat 'Oh, aye. It's terrible. It seems folk would rather be burned these days than planted.'

'Hand it over,' Jed said, grimly.

'What are you gonna do with it?' Omo asked as Jed pocketed the balance of his fee.

'Give it to the community centre. We'll be putting something back, for the kiddies. Just like you said. Remember?' Omo nodded miserably. 'And if I'm late for this wedding I'll throttle the pair of you!'

The cab drew up at the register office and Jed jumped out before it had even come to a halt, followed by the other two.

'How!' the cabbie yelled. 'Who's settling up?'

'Oh, lad alive,' Omo moaned, dipping into his pocket. 'Talk about rubbing salt in.'

Inside, Emma was pacing up and down, exchanging worried glances with Pep and looking at her watch. She turned anxiously as Mary came in, with Bob and the two kids. Mary immediately went up to her. 'I didn't want to be here,' she said quietly, 'but Pep insisted and the kids wanted to see their dad wed.'

'It's fine, Mary.' Emma looked radiant. She didn't intend to let anything Pep did spoil her day. 'Really, don't worry.' She squeezed Mary's hand reassuringly and looked at her watch again. 'I should never have let him have the bottle of vodka,' she muttered.

At that moment Jed burst through the doors to cheers from the assembled throng. 'I'm really sorry,' he panted to Emma. 'Not my fault, I can explain—'

'Not now, thank you. Later.' She turned to Beckie. 'Are you ready, pet?'

'Are you?' Beckie asked innocently.

Emma chose not to answer but took her daughter's hand and, standing tall, nodded to Pep. 'Let's go then, shall we?' She slipped her arm through Jed's and with Beckie following behind set off to be married.

About a hundred guests grew steadily drunk on Pep's champagne. After the ceremony, as the confetti had rained down on the couple, Jed had hugged his sister. 'Good luck,' he said. He then offered his hand to Pep, who embraced him instead.

'Brothers-in-law,' Pep said, emotionally.

'Right,' Jed agreed.

'And a clean start, eh? What do you say?' Jed had said nothing.

Now he was sitting next to Wendy on the top table. 'Thanks,' he said.

'I'm here for the song,' Wendy replied.

'Does this mean I'm gonna have to write a song every time I want to take you out?'

'Quite possibly.'

He laughed. 'It could be a bloody long courtship!'

Music, dancing and noisy conversation soon took over from eating. Big Chrissie sidled up to Archie. 'Bit of a change from last night,' he said, nodding towards Pep, who was dancing with his new bride.

'That night's not over yet,' Archie said, nodding towards the door and two girls who had just walked through it. 'Them's the two lassies Pep was grabbing hold of last night, are they not?'

'Last night?' Omo said. 'Don't ask me. My head was full of charitable thoughts.'

'Yeah.' Chrissie nodded. 'That's them.'

'Incredible,' Archie marvelled. 'The front of the man.'

Jed had seen the women, too. 'What the hell are they doing here?' he mumbled. As the band finished their tune he stood up to throw them out, but the singer obviously decided now was time to make his special announcement. He tapped the microphone.

'Ladies and gentlemen, we've come to a very special part of the evening. It's a real thrill for me to be able to ask Jed Shepperd up onto the stage. Jed?'

The whole party roared their approval and Jed had no choice but to jump on the stage and strap on his guitar. He walked nervously to the microphone. 'Hello,' he said and the friendly crowd cheered again as he strummed a few chords and checked his sound levels. 'It's been a while,' he said. 'Can you hear me at the back?'

'No!' a voice responded. 'Turn it up!'

'I've not written anything for a long time, or so it seems, but this is for you, Emma, and for Beckie.' The band started up and Jed began to sing 'Blue Roses', a song that perfectly captured the moment. As Emma danced with Pep, Archie took Beckie onto the floor and Omo and Big Chrissie were dragged out by their wives.

Jed was almost lost in the lyrics, enjoying the response of the audience, when he glanced up and saw Alan Clarke arriving, accompanied by

Lucy. They both stood at the back, listening intently. Alan gave him a thumbs-up and pointed to Lucy, who smiled hello. Jed's heart sank into his boots. He looked across at Wendy, who had also seen the new arrivals. She stood up and mouthed, 'You fucking shit' at Jed before walking out. Unable to break off from singing for his sister, Jed could do nothing but watch her go. The moment the song was over the crowd went wild with enthusiasm. Jed gave them a wave and tried to get after Wendy, but Emma came up with tears in her eyes and hugged him.

'That was so lovely, Jed.'

'Thanks, Emm . . .'

'Surprise,' Clarke mouthed to him across the crowd.

'Too right,' Jed mouthed back, and left the room.

'Congratulations, Emma,' Clarke said when he managed to reach her. 'I'm Alan Clarke. I used to work at Jed's record company, but please don't hold it against me.' He handed her a gift-wrapped Tiffany box. 'Little something for the bride. I hope you don't mind Lucy and me crashing your party like this.'

'Oh . . .' Emma suddenly realised what was happening. 'You're Lucy are you? Adrian's sister?'

'That's right.'

'Haven't you met?' Clarke was surprised.

'Not until today,' Emma told him.

'Congratulations,' Lucy said.

'Thank you.'

'Excuse me, would you?' Lucy headed off after Jed.

'When Lucy told me Jed was gonna play a new song,' Clarke explained, 'I just had to be here to hear it. And what a song, eh?'

Outside, Lucy found Jed watching a taxi disappearing into the night. 'She's easily upset, that girl,' she said.

'No she's not,' Jed replied. 'She just saw you and me in the same room and assumed we were together.'

'I'm glad to hear you tell her as little as you tell me.'

'What are you doing here, anyway?'

'Alan's asked me to work for him.' She smiled. 'When I went along to see him we got to talking. About you, mostly. And it seemed like a really good idea. He's up here with a plan, Jed.'

Jed made his way back into the hall after her and joined Clarke and Emma. 'Congratulations, Jed,' Alan said. 'I hope there's more songs where that one came from?'

'So do I,' Jed muttered.

'Did Lucy tell you about her and me?'

'Yeah.'

'Great, eh?'

'Oh, terrific!' Jed was not sure quite what was going on.

Pep came across to join them. 'Nice tune, Jed.' He turned to Emma. 'We should cut the cake, pet.'

'You don't have a problem with Lucy, do you?' Alan asked when they were alone.

'I don't.' Jed paused. 'I just wish you'd let me know you were coming.'

'I didn't know myself until this morning. Managed to get a room, though – here. Same hotel. Seems like this break was just what you needed to get the old creative juices flowing again.'

Jed shook his head. 'I think about the mess I'm in with Paradigm and I wonder if there's any point. Did Lucy tell you about the meeting?'

'That's why I'm here. I'd like to talk to you, Jed.'

'That's what we're doing, isn't it?'

'I mean a serious talk. I want to sign you to my label.'

'Your label?' Jed was startled.

'My label.' Jed's next question was drowned by a cheer. They turned to see Pep and Emma cut the cake and then heard a crash as a fight started at the bar. Jed glanced at his watch. 'Right on cue. Slow dance, get pissed, cut the cake and then the punch-up. It's traditional.' The fight quickly spread as others piled in and chairs flew round the room.

'It's a different world,' Clarke marvelled.

'It's the *real* world,' Jed corrected him as the band struck up a tune and everyone went back to dancing.

Jed and Alan made their way up onto a first-floor balcony where it was quiet enough for Alan to lay out his plans. 'I could offer you a small advance,' he said, 'enough to cover your immediate problems, plus as much studio time and space as you want. Where you want. Up here or down the road.'

'It sounds really appealing, Alan,' Jed admitted, 'but contractually I'm stuck. Tied in knots. It's a big, aggressive, messy can of worms. You should know. You did it.'

Clarke nodded ruefully. 'What if I could untangle it all, without any aggro for you?' he asked.

'How's Warren Bowles going to feel about that?' Jed asked.

'What does it matter?' Clarke didn't understand.

'He's been trying to get me a management deal.'

'That's not what I heard.' Alan was surprised.

'What did you hear?'

'I heard he's been warning everybody off you. Telling them you're poison.'

'Why on earth would he want to do that?' Now it was Jed's turn to be surprised.

'Good question.'

Emma was waiting for her new husband in the honeymoon suite. She was wearing the most exotic lingerie she had ever possessed and had laid out the top tier of the wedding cake, a bottle of champagne and two glasses on a small side table. Just as she glanced at her watch there was the sound of a card key going into the slot and the door opened. Pep walked in smiling, followed by the two girls, both of whom were obviously drunk. Emma stood, momentarily speechless.

'We're gonna need some more glasses, pet,' Pep said.

'You bastard!' Emma shouted. 'Get these two sluts out of here!'

'Slut?' One of the girls giggled. 'Hey, you're the one in the skimpy nightie.'

'These are my guests, Emma,' Pep said. 'Our guests!'

Emma launched herself at the girls. 'Out! Out, out, *out*!' The two women scurried quickly through the door. Emma turned on Pep. 'How dare you? How could you? After everything you said, after everything I believed?'

'You shouldn't have done that, Emma,' Pep said coldly.

'Damn right I shouldn't. I should never have married you. Jesus, I've been such a bloody fool!'

'You've humiliated me,' Pep continued as if she hadn't spoken, 'in front of my guests. I invite them up to my hotel room for a drink, which I'm paying for—'

'Jed was right,' Emma snapped.

'Jed!' Pep's eyes widened with fury. 'Ah, so it's him, is it, who's been filling your head with shit? I'll give you "Jed"!' He lunged for her and grabbed her throat. 'Where is he now, then, eh? When you need him? Your darling brother? Jed!'

They fell together over the side table, sending the cake and champagne flying. Pep was on top of her, blinded with drunken rage. '"Here comes the bride . . ."' he sang as he squeezed hard on her throat. Emma was choking, gasping, trying to scream, her arms thrashing in a desperate struggle to break free of his tightening, throttling grip. Then she felt something cold and metallic, as her fingers closed on the ornate cake knife.

'You could sign to another big label,' Clarke was saying to Jed. 'But I can't imagine you'd be too keen on going down that road again.'

The two men had continued their conversation in Alan's room, just down the corridor, Jed had noticed, from the honeymoon suite.

'You'd be right,' Jed agreed.

'I realise there's a potential conflict of interests, me being both the manager and the record company, but at least we'd cut out the middleman, and you could always give me a cuff if I got out of line.'

'You're making it sound very tempting, Alan.'

'I'm trying to, Jed. What do you say?'

As Jed opened his mouth to reply a terrible scream echoed down the hallway. He immediately knew it was his sister's voice. They both rushed into the corridor. By the time they got to the door of the honeymoon suite Emma was standing, frozen with fear. Jed looked past her to the body lying on the floor with the cake knife still embedded in his side.

It was obvious that Pep was dead.

CHAPTER EIGHTEEN

'Mrs Peploe,' the magistrate said, not un-kindly, 'this is the first step in your trial procedure which, due to the nature of the crime, must be tried by the Crown Court. Do you understand that?' Emma nodded from the dock. 'Do you have legal representation?'

'Yes.' Emma spoke quietly. 'I believe so.'

'Neil Fawdington, ma'am.' A slightly flustered young lawyer stood up and addressed the bench, his case notes in his hand, 'I'm representing Mrs Peploe – as of this morning, I'm afraid. Just trying to get up to speed.'

'Is Mrs Peploe aware of the procedures, and how to plead?' the magistrate asked.

'Not quite as yet, ma'am.'

She raised an eyebrow. 'Let's delay any plea until you've had enough time to talk to your client then, shall we?'

'On behalf of my client, can I say thank you very much, ma'am.'

'Prosecution.' The magistrate turned to the other side.

'Good morning, ma'am.' A confident, clinical looking man stood up. 'The prosecution will be seeking a maximum sentence for this, a premeditated and ruthless attack on a well-respected and high-standing member of the community.'

The magistrate read through the case notes again. 'I see you have a young daughter, Mrs Peploe.'

'Yes, Your Honour,' Emma replied, 'Beckie.' Fawdington leaned over and whispered something to her. 'Sorry,' Emma corrected herself, 'Your Worship.'

'I cannot grant you bail, Mrs Peploe, due to the very serious nature of the alleged offence. You will be remanded in custody for seven days and the case will be referred to Newcastle Crown Court.'

'Right,' Emma said, matter-of-factly, 'thank you.' She looked round at the public seats at the back of the courtroom. Jed gave a reassuring smile.

'Good luck,' the magistrate said, as Emma was led away.

'Thanks,' Emma replied and Jed was amazed by how calm she seemed.

'Five minutes, all right?' the policeman asked, letting him into a room where Emma sat, alone, behind a perspex panel.

'Thanks.' Jed sat down and the policeman wandered off to the other end of the room. 'What a mess,' he said.

'It'll get sorted,' Emma reassured him. 'How's Beckie?'

'She's fine. Wonders where her mam is, but other than that . . .'

'Could you bring me some stuff over to the prison, Jed? Some underwear and some make-up, and a nice party dress. I want to look decent next time I'm in that court.'

'Yes, of course, anything else?'

'A picture of Beckie. There's one on my dressing table in the bedroom.'

'I'll get it all today for you.'

'Don't let the social services people take her away, Jed.'

'No, no, course not. She'll stay with me, until . . . there shouldn't be a problem. I am the bairn's uncle, after all.'

'Thanks.'

'And I'm gonna have a word with your solicitor fella, Mr Fawdington. Make sure he's got all the facts. Make sure he knows about everything.' The policeman cleared his throat and tapped his watch. 'Got to go,' Jed said.

'Durham Jail!' Emma shuddered.

'You shouldn't feel bad about what happened, Emm.'

'I don't. I'm glad I did it.' Jed was startled by her words but, before he could say any more, a uniformed arm reached in and led his little sister away. As he stood up to go he felt close to tears.

When the school bell rang to announce the end of the day, Beckie rushed out to where Jed was standing, a few yards away from the other parents. 'Hello, darling,' he greeted her.

'Uncle Jed, where's prison?' she asked.

'Why do you ask that, pet?'

'Pamela Johnson said that's where my mam's going to live.'

'Howway,' Jed sighed and picked her up. 'Let's get you home. What would you like for your tea?'

'Treats.'

As they walked off he tickled her and she giggled, distracted from the other mums who were whispering among themselves about the pop star in their midst, whose sister had just killed her new husband.

Alan Clarke looked expectantly at the figure of Dick Pilsbury at Paradigm's London offices. He had decided to start the ball rolling. 'You want to buy out Jed Shepperd's contract?' Pilsbury clarified, shuffling through the piles of paperwork in front of him. 'A rather ambitious move for a fledgling independent, isn't it?'

'Is it?' Alan seemed very cool.

'We'd be talking lots of lolly. You know how it is.'

'Mmm.' Alan nodded. 'You take a piece of Jed's arse, to fund things like all your overseas offices, regardless of whether or not his records have been released in those territories, and that he himself will probably never go there.'

Pilsbury raised his finger. 'May go there. You never know in this game. We have to take the global overview, Alan, whereas indies like yourself tend to think nationally. Provincially. Which is understandable.'

'From little acorns . . .' Alan reminded him.

'I seem to recall that the Paradigm organisation started out selling sewing machines from a back yard in Tokyo.'

'That was a long time ago. We've come a long way since then.'

'Just do your sums. Let me know the figure. 'Cause from now, Jed's product will be going through me.'

'Shouldn't I be hearing this from Jed's management?' Pilsbury asked.

'You are.'

'Really?' he looked surprised. 'Well, that's his decision, I suppose.'

'That's right. But all the other decisions are mine, and the first one is already made. I'll be looking to audit. See what's been lost, or hidden, inside the machine.'

Alan noticed the look of disquiet which flitted across Pilsbury's normally bland features.

Bowles was at his apartment, having an uncomfortable meeting with Connors and McClusky, when Pilsbury's call came. The call got through immediately, Bowles found himself musing, despite the fact that a couple of telephone engineers seemed to have set up permanent camp in a tent on the pavement outside the block.

'Was he serious?' he asked Pilsbury.

'I presume so,' Pilsbury's voice said through the loudspeaker. 'Clarke was never a wind-up merchant.'

'Can you ignore him?' Bowles asked.

'That's going to be difficult if he puts in a formal

offer. Even if we ignore him on this one, we'd still have to deal with him as a manager.'

'He's managing Jed?' Bowles was surprised.

'He is. And he wants to audit. I wonder who put that into his head?'

'Don't be sarcastic, Dicky,' Bowles warned. 'I don't like it.'

'I don't like it either.' Pilsbury's voice betrayed his growing panic. 'You promised me it would never get this bad.'

'Maybe it's time for a career change.' Bowles cut off the phone and turned to Connors and McClusky. 'Any suggestions?' he asked.

'I could take Clarke out,' Connors said, looking increasingly manic. McClusky looked horrified.

'That only delays the problem,' Bowles said. 'It doesn't solve it.'

Connors smiled slowly. 'Take out Jed?'

'That would be the cleanest way,' Bowles agreed.

'How about we take them both out?' Connors became even more excited.

'Even cleaner,' Bowles approved.

'What is this?' McClusky was incredulous. 'It's Wednesday, so let's kill somebody?'

'It's Monday, actually,' Bowles corrected him.

'You can't just murder everyone!' McClusky protested.

'Why not?' Connors asked. 'There's no connection. The police think that Adrian Lynn's death was suicide. The German bird's down as a drug overdose, and that happened in Germany, I seem to recall.' He grinned. 'I don't see a problem.'

'You can't keep topping people in Britain,' the detective argued, 'and hope that I'm going to be in charge of the investigation! Sooner or later it's gonna lead back to your doorstep and there's gonna be shit all over it.'

'What would you do, Detective Inspector, in your infinite wisdom?' Bowles enquired.

'I'm not calling the shots here.' McClusky was backing down. 'You are.'

'That's right, old chap,' Bowles purred. 'Don't forget it.' He threw the policeman an envelope. As it landed on his lap some fifty pound notes spilled out. McClusky pushed them back in and left without another word.

'How about I kill him as well?' Connors suggested once McClusky had gone.

'They don't like it,' Bowles said, shaking his head, 'when you kill a copper.'

'I know.' Connors grinned.

'Priorities. Get up to Newcastle and take care of Shepperd first. Make it look like an accident. We'll worry about Alan Clarke and PC Plod later.'

'Oh, goody!' Connors grinned malevolently.

Wendy was sitting on the floor of her living room, sifting through a bundle of old classic LPs when the bell went. She glanced at her watch. A bit late for callers, she thought. She opened the door to find Jed standing on the doorstep, Beckie asleep on his shoulder.

'Wha—' she began, but Jed put a finger to his lips, then pointed to his sleeping burden.

Crocodile Shoes

'Can we come in?' he whispered. 'Please?'

For a moment she stood her ground. She was furious at the nerve of the man. But then she relented and stepped aside to let them past, closing the door quietly behind them.

CHAPTER NINETEEN

The reception area of Colville and Long was impressive, but as the young woman led Jed further and further through the labyrinth, first past opulent partners' offices, then past the tea room and washing-up area, he began to feel less confident. Eventually they turned into a small corridor, walked past piles of stationery and came to a small office next to the toilet. The young woman knocked.

'Hello?' Neil Fawdington's voice came from inside. The woman opened the door and ushered Jed into a small room filled with piles of unruly paperwork. Fawdington sat in the middle of it all looking flummoxed and confused. He stood up to greet Jed. 'Ah, Mr Shepperd, come in. Excuse the mess, but I've got rather a lot on. The trials and tribulations of being a junior partner.'

'You're a partner?' Jed was surprised.

'Well, not quite, not yet. A junior.'

'The court appointed you specifically, did it?' Jed was feeling less and less easy about the situation.

'Not specifically, no.' Fawdington became defensive. 'This firm has an obligation to supply the city with defence solicitors.'

'An obligation?' Jed queried. 'You mean a contract?'

'If you like. It's not the most profitable side of the firm, I can assure you.'

'I'm not feeling very assured, Mr Fawdington.'

'Nor am I,' Fawdington admitted. 'Mrs Shepperd is in a serious pickle.'

'It's Mrs Peploe,' Jed corrected him.

'I'm sorry?'

'My sister's name. It's Peploe, not Shepperd. She was married.'

'Of course she was.' He checked his papers. 'Almost missed it there. Mind you, it must go down as one of the shortest marriages in history though, eh?' He chuckled and then saw Jed wasn't laughing. 'And one of the most tragic, of course,' he added.

'So,' Jed said hopefully, 'what is your plan?'

'It's very open and shut. She . . . Mrs Peploe had the knife. Mrs Peploe was the only one there, and *Mr* Peploe died as a result of a fatal stab wound to the heart. Guilty.'

'But it was self-defence,' Jed protested. 'He was trying to kill her.'

'Two people, one knife. Mr Peploe wasn't armed.'

'But he was beating the shit out of her. Look, get me into the witness box. I was there. I'll tell the jury what happened.'

'But you *weren't* there, were you?' Fawdington put on his best cross-examination voice. 'In the room. You didn't actually see what happened, did you?'

200

'What? Do you think I'd come in here and make all of this up?'

'It wouldn't be the first time.' Jed couldn't believe what he was hearing. 'What we do,' the young solicitor went on, 'is enter a plea of guilty and then, just before sentence is passed, I will tell Their Worships all about the mitigating circumstances. That's how it's done.'

'Have you ever done this before?' Jed asked as the horrible truth dawned on him.

'Not all on my own like this,' Neil said, excitedly. 'Don't worry, Mr Shepperd. I assure you my speech will be memorable. It will be an impassioned plea, a cry from the heart for the court to be lenient and merciful when sentencing your sister.'

'Isn't that leaving it a bit late?' Jed suggested.

'Mr Shepperd,' Fawdington said, mustering all the dignity he could find, 'I don't tell you how to make records – please don't tell me how to conduct a defence. With a bit of luck and a fair wind we'll get your sister off with about eight years.'

His words hit Jed like a punch on the chin.

'I can't allow this to carry on,' Jed said as Wendy arranged fish fingers and peas into a smiley face on a plate. 'The guy's a bloody teaboy, for God's sake. His first ride without stabilisers and he wants to be Perry Mason.'

Wendy put the smiling plate in front of Beckie. 'You need a proper criminal lawyer,' she agreed, 'someone with experience and a proven track record.'

'Do you know how much a top-notch criminal lawyer's going to cost?'

'What about talking to Alan Clarke?' Wendy suggested. 'Maybe you should take him up on his offer.'

'Actually,' Jed admitted, 'I *have* taken him up on his offer.'

'Oh.' Wendy was surprised not to have been told. 'Right.'

'But he can't help me out here. I need money for this and it's the one thing I can't get my hands on.' He took a breath. 'I could ask Lucy . . .' Wendy shot him a look that suggested he should think again. 'I could do a gig,' he said after a moment's thought.

'What, like a benefit?'

'Yeah. They have my arse in a sling recording-wise, but they don't own me live!' His enthusiasm suddenly gave way to nerves. 'But where would I start?'

'Right here,' Wendy told him. 'We can do it together.' She gave his hand a little squeeze of encouragement.

'I'll need a band, and some place to rehearse. I wonder if my friend the vicar would give us her church hall.'

'I don't see why not.'

'I'll get on to Alan and Lucy for some management back-up.' But this second mention of Lucy's name sent Wendy stalking out of the room.

'The Lord is my shepherd. I shall not want,' Jed read, looking down occasionally at his niece tucked up in the bed. 'He maketh me to lie down in green pastures. He leadeth me beside the still waters. He restoreth my soul. He leadeth me in the paths of righteousness for his name's sake. Yea, though I walk through the valley of the shadow of death, I shall fear no evil, for Thou art with me. Thy rod and Thy staff, they comfort me.' He closed the Bible. 'That's enough for tonight. Sleepy time up north.'

'Uncle Jed?' she said.

'Yes, pet?'

'Can we say a prayer for me mam?'

'Of course we can.' He closed his eyes and put his hands together and Beckie copied him.

'Dear Jesus,' she said, 'please look after my mam, wherever she is. I'm sure you can see her, from up there in heaven. Please don't listen to what Pamela Johnson says. All them nasty things. She's telling fibs. My mam's lovely. Please let her come home soon. I don't like it when she's not here. Amen.'

Jed opened his eyes and saw a tear squeezing out from under Beckie's screwed up lids. He took a deep breath to stop himself choking too. 'Amen,' he said, gently stroking her forehead.

Once she had got to sleep Jed took the Bible downstairs and began to flip through it, remembering passages he had read as a child. '. . . And yea, though I walk through the valley of the shadow of death, I will fear no evil, for thou art with me. Thy rod and Thy staff comfort me . . .' Putting down the book, he picked up his guitar and began to work on some chord sequences.

*   *   *

Connors was restless. He'd been sitting here for what seemed like hours watching the house from his car. He peered again at the windows. The upstairs one was still lit. Little brat's bedtime, no doubt. It was that time of day.

Then the light went off and a minute later a silhouette became visible in the lower room. Shepperd.

Won't be long now, he thought, and gave the car's interior the benefit of his evil little chuckle. Won't be long now.

The next day Jed was still working on the song, trying out different lyrics. He'd decided to call the song 'Fear of Evil'.

'Jed,' Wendy said, obviously restless.

'Yes?' Jed answered, although he was lost in his own world.

'Have you thought what we're going to do after the trial, when all this is over?'

'I can't think about us right now, Wendy,' he said. 'I'm surprised at you.'

'I didn't mean us, Jed. What if Emma does get a lengthy prison sentence? It's looking increasingly likely. I don't mind you telling the social services people that this is your house.' Jed looked guilty. 'And that I'm your housekeeper.' He looked even more guilty. 'But what happens to Beckie then?'

'We could get married,' he suggested, 'and adopt her.' He laughed, but he was only half pretending. She laughed too. 'Anyway,' he said, 'right now we've got a gig to organise.'

For the next few days their feet hardly touched the ground as they hustled rental stores for equipment, the band from the wedding for back-up music and truck companies for transport. The Reverend Kate was happy to let them have the church hall for their rehearsals, but none of the music venues in the city were willing to cut their prices for the gig itself.

'They all think you're loaded,' Wendy told Jed and the young vicar after she had given up trying to talk the last one on her list into taking them on. 'That's the problem.'

'If I was loaded,' Jed complained, 'I'd hardly be on the beg, would I?'

'The venues all say they'd like to help but they can't do it for free. They're all owned by big parent companies. Then there's the insurance.'

'How much?' Jed asked.

'The cheapest was three grand. The others all wanted a cut of the door.'

'The mean bastards! They must know we're potless. It's a benefit concert, for God's sake.' He looked up and saw what might have been a mildly reproving smile on Kate's face. 'Sorry.'

Kate shook her head, unworried. 'How much do you need?' she asked.

'Three thousand pounds,' Wendy told her. 'Minimum.'

'If we had that kind of money we could pay for the bloody barrister!' Jed exploded.

'I think the church can cover that,' Kate said. 'It's a good investment – if we were to get a return of, say, ten per cent.'

Jed stared at her in amazement and then broke into a smile. 'You're on!' He turned to Wendy. 'Blimey, who'd have thought it? Jed Shepperd in concert, presented by Saint Aidan's Parish Church!'

'We're not out of the woods yet,' Wendy warned. 'Unless we can tell the whole town you're back, all this won't mean a thing. We need to promote.'

An hour later Jed was on the phone to Alan Clarke at the new offices of Criminal Records. 'I wish I could make it easier for you,' Alan said, 'but right now, you know how things stand. All I can give you is names and phone numbers. And put Lucy on a train.'

'Er, no, Alan,' Jed said quickly. 'We, er, don't need that much help, just yet. Thank you.'

'Is Lucy being part of our team a problem, Jed?' Alan asked.

'No.' Jed swallowed hard. 'No, not at all! Any news from that two-faced bastard Bowles?'

'No, I can't figure the guy out. I can't see what he could gain from slagging you off . . . Listen, I know a good guy in radio up there. You got a pen handy?'

The radio station was Beacon Radio and the name Jed had been given was that of Bill Bowry, a large grizzled DJ whose mellifluous tones conjured up a very different picture in the minds of his audience. 'Jed Shepperd,' he announced to the listening public, 'our very own local hero, took his music around the world, and now he's back, with a benefit gig on Saturday night right here in the city. And the man himself is here with us tonight, in person, on Bill Bowry's talk-line, to tell us all about it. Jed, welcome to Beacon Radio.'

Jed felt nervous. Jed Shepperd – the man who had been in hundreds of radio stations, local, regional, national, and had been interviewed by presenters, DJs, chat-show hosts, the famous, the not so famous and the downright notorious – was nervous.

But why? Why now, sitting in this little studio, the big DJ looking at him from his studio desk festooned with dials and faders, surrounded by gram decks, CD players and cartridge machines?

'Hello . . .' He cleared his throat. Yes, he was nervous. 'Er, hello, er . . . Bill.'

'A benefit concert. For who, Jed?'

'Well, we're trying to raise money for various causes. Both here at home and abroad. There's a church-based fund, for the kids in Bosnia, so we'll try and give something to them.'

'And what about nearer home?' Bill coaxed.

'It's a bit difficult to talk about in detail, Bill, for legal reasons.'

'Well, it's no secret that your sister is in a bit of trouble, Jed. The papers have been full of nothing else for days, now. If I said that some of the proceeds from your concert would be going towards a fighting fund, a defence war-chest . . .'

'I wouldn't argue with you,' Jed said.

'OK, Jed. I think we get the picture. What kind of stuff are you gonna be playing? What can folk expect if they come along? When they come along? All the old hits?'

'Yes.'

'And some new songs?'

Jed's nerves were getting worse instead of better as the interview progressed. 'Yes.'

'Really?' Bill became excited. 'So there'll be an exclusive opportunity to hear you perform your new material, first time out of the bag, so to speak?'

'That's right.'

'And what kind of songs can the good people out there expect to hear, Jed? Is it the same Jed Shepperd? "Cowboy Dreams"? "Crocodile Shoes"?'

'Well' – Jed squirmed in his seat uncomfortably – 'it's changed a bit . . . I've changed a bit, these past couple of years. I think the new stuff reflects that. I hope it does.'

'And you're gonna play a song for us tonight, right?'

'That's right.'

'A new song?'

'Yeah, brand new.'

Bill gave Jed the thumbs-up and he walked across the studio to the sound booth where his band was waiting for him. 'So here is it, folks,' Bill announced as he watched the singer strap on his guitar, 'the first new song for all of two years from our own Jed Shepperd. And don't forget to tell your friends where you heard it first – Beacon ninety-eight point six.'

'This song,' Jed told the listeners once he had

made himself comfortable, 'is called "Fear No Evil". I'm playing it for my sister. I hope you can hear it, Emma. Keep your chin up.' And after four bars of intro music, Jed began to sing.

When the world is dark, when the lights
    go down,
when the demons walk, when they're all
    around,
there's a light that comes from a place on
    high –
there's a light that comes that the angels
    shine –
and it shines for you, and it shines for me,
and it shines for all, and it shines for free.
When the world is dark, when the demons
    walk,
there's a light that shines like a burning arc;
and though I walk through the valley of the
    shadow
I will fear no evil;
and though I walk through the valley of the
    shadow
I will fear no evil.
Since the dawn of time, when the world
    began,
we've borne witness to all the acts of man –
how he ruled the earth, when he learned
    to walk,
how he learned to hurt, when he learned
    to talk –
and he's broken laws, and he's broken
    dreams,

and he's broken bones, and ignored the
   screams.
Through the longest day, through the
   darkest night,
there will always shine, His redeeming light.'

Miles apart, in two very different rooms, two
women – each in her own world, each with
her own very special thoughts – listened to the
words of Jed Shepperd's song. In a small cell on
the remand wing of Durham jail, a woman on a
murder charge looked at a picture of her small
daughter, which stood on a cabinet by the pillow
of her functional bed. The song ended, but she
didn't hear the smooth tones of the DJ. She was
lost in her thoughts.

In a house that might have been a universe
away, Mary sat, listening, perched on the edge
of her armchair with her head in her hands. As
the song ended Bob dropped his paper.

'You're gonna have to make your mind up,
love,' he told his wife, 'one way or the other.'

Mary nodded.

CHAPTER TWENTY

Mary tried to speak to Jed the next day. She got as far as creeping up to the church hall where he and the band were rehearsing, she even peeked in through the window at them. She paced around for a few moments, trying to pluck up the courage to go in and talk to him.

'Sorry lads,' she heard Jed shout to the others inside. She saw him dump his guitar and grab his coat. 'Got a date. Gotta go.'

She hurried away quickly, hoping he hadn't seen her run down to the end of the alley. She felt frightened and disappointed with herself.

Mums were congregating at the school gates, when Jed ran up and took his place. He looked around and scratched his head. There was no sign of Beckie. Just as he was about to become worried she emerged with a man.

'Mr Shepperd,' the man said, recognising him. 'I'm Ivan, Beckie's playgroup leader.' They shook hands. 'I've got some good news and some bad news. Which do you want first?'

'Let's get the bad bit out of the way,' Jed suggested.

'Beckie's got nits,' Ivan said, lowering his voice

and glancing at Beckie to confirm that she hadn't heard. Jed immediately scratched his head again. 'Don't feel too bad about it – there's an epidemic. Every kid in the school's crawling. It's just about impossible to avoid.'

'That explains why I've been scratching my head so often lately,' Jed said. 'And the good news?'

'We had a whip-round in the staff room.' He passed Jed an envelope. 'It's not a huge amount, but I hope it helps.'

'Every little bit helps. Thanks very much.'

'Everyone here likes Emma – sympathises. We see a lot of that stuff, mothers turning up at the gates with black eyes and cut lips. It's difficult to know just what to do. Anyway . . .'

'Thanks,' Jed said again. 'And thanks on behalf of Emma. Hopefully, she'll be able to thank you all herself before too long.'

'Fingers crossed on that one.'

Connors sat in his car, watching as Shepperd talked to the chap from the school, watching as Shepperd and the girl crossed the road, Shepperd scratching his head hard. He started the engine and prepared to move off, just as a minibus doubled parked in front of him and a gaggle of older schoolchildren got off.

'Sooner or later, Shepperd,' he muttered angrily to himself as Jed and Beckie disappeared from sight. 'Sooner or later.'

Saturday. The night of the concert. Jed bounced

onto the small stage. Several thousand people
were packed into the venue. The set was spartan,
with no frills, but the music was raw, tight,
powerful and rock-solid. Everyone was having a
good time. Jed had stopped scratching his head,
but now there was a new irritation: the smell of
the special shampoo he'd bought yesterday after
picking Beckie up from school. He'd lathered
both their heads with the foul-smelling concoc-
tion, and the stink had remained with him all
day. He tried not to think about it as he launched
into 'Country Boy'.

'Thank you very much,' Jed said as he finished
the song. 'I'm not a great one for words, outside
of the songs, but I just want to say thank you
for turning up on such a cold night and at such
short notice. I'm surprised anybody remembered
who I was!' The audience cheered and he smiled
happily. 'This next song was inspired by two men
I recently shared a cell with. It's called "I Refuse
To Lie Down", and if we make enough of a racket,
who knows, they might just hear it!'

Matt, the photographer, was running and jumping around the front of the hall, shooting everything that was happening on stage, capturing
every moment. Everyone's eyes were on Jed and
the band, nobody noticed Connors making his
way from the back of the hall to the side of the
stage. A few minutes later he was in the wings,
merging with all the other liggers.

Connors could see Jed on stage and could see
that the lead from his mike trailed back, ending
at the mixing console just beyond him. He picked

up a small lamp and wrenched the wires out, moving casually with them to the back of the console.

From the front of house Matt noticed the strange man at the side of the stage. Something about him didn't look right. He decided to get a better view, and focused his telephoto lens onto him.

Jed had the mike in his hand as Connors identified the right jackplug and moved the live leads to it, just as a massive hand grabbed him. 'What are you doing, man?' Shit! One of the bloody roadies.

'This was lying down here.' Connors held up the live cable. 'I thought it had fallen out. I was gonna plug it back in.'

'You could've killed somebody,' the roadie told him, shouting over the din.

'Oh dear,' Connors shouted. 'We don't want people getting killed, do we?'

'Who are you, anyway? What are you doing back here?' The roadie's suspicions were roused now and Connors knew it was time to go. He pushed the live wires into the man's open palm. As the electricity shot into him the man shuddered and was thrown to the floor, stunned. Connors disappeared as others came to the stricken roadie's assistance.

On stage, Jed felt happy. He felt he had come home, in more ways than one. When the band struck up 'Crocodile Shoes' the whole place erupted in front of him.

Backstage, after the concert, everyone came round to celebrate with the star. Jed, euphoric at the way the evening had gone, climbed on a chair and called for order. 'I just want to say a few words of thanks to all of you who've worked your bollocks off' – he spotted the Reverend Kate in the party and gulped – 'or whatever. You've all worked hard, for nothing, to put tonight together. So I thank you for that.'

'It was worth it to see you up there, Jed,' Omo said, 'poncing about on that stage.'

'I also want to thank you on behalf of Emma, my sister. She's in a terrible jam right now. I've been praying for her and that didn't come naturally to a lifelong unbeliever like myself, but I'm giving it a pop. And I have to say, it doesn't feel as bad as I thought it would.' He raised his glass. 'Here's to Emma. May God keep an eye out for her.' Kate smiled as they all raised their glasses, but she could see that some of the lads were looking a bit worried. 'Now carry on getting pissed – you deserve it.'

Omo noticed that Kate, probably not used to more than the odd cream sherry, was starting to sway merrily. 'I don't suppose you can get much, in your line, eh?' he said, by way of a subtle opening line.

'Much of what?' Kate enquired, innocently.

'Y'know – satisfaction.' He winked and Kate got the idea.

'I get more satisfaction than you could ever imagine,' she smiled.

'Yeah?' Omo was surprised.

'Really. In all kinds of different ways and in the most surprising of places.'

'Really?' He was intrigued.

'Absolutely!'

'Are priests allowed to have dates?' he enquired boldly.

'No.' His face fell. 'But vicars can.'

'What brand are you?'

'Vicar.' She grinned naughtily.

'Maybe you and me could, er, spend a bit of time together, y'know, like' – he raised an eyebrow – 'together.'

'We'd love to see you down at the church.' Kate assured him. 'The doors are always open.'

'Are they?' That news genuinely worried him. 'That could be a big mistake.'

Kate wandered over to Jed – who was talking to Chrissie – leaving Omo confused.

'You had me going there, for a minute,' Chrissie was telling Jed. 'I thought you'd turned into Cliff Richard!'

'Not yet,' Jed said, turning to Kate. 'Mind, if Emma gets to walk away from this, I'll start believing that miracles really can happen.'

'And prayers really can be answered?' Kate asked.

Omo joined them. 'If he could dae that trick out of the Bible where they turned all the water into wine, we could all make a fortune!'

A bouncer came over. 'Jed, there's a woman out the back wants a word. She says she's an old friend.'

'Hey up, lads,' Archie teased, 'the groupies have arrived!'

'That really would be a miracle,' Omo added.

Jed followed the man to the door, where two more bouncers were keeping the reporters out. 'Mary?' He was startled to see her. 'She's a friend, lads. Could you let her in?' They parted to let Mary through, closing the gap the minute she was inside. 'We're all having a drink through the back, there,' Jed said.

'I don't want to come to your party, Jed,' Mary said. 'I need to have a word with you. Alone.'

'Is everything all right?' Jed was alarmed by the expression on her face.

'No.' She shook her head.

Taking her by the hand he led her out onto the empty stage. The main venue was deserted, nothing left behind but the rubbish the crowd had dropped. 'Quietest place in the whole auditorium,' he said, grabbing a couple of tall stools that had been used in the show.

'It's about Emma,' Mary said, once she was sitting down. 'Well, it's about Pep, really.'

'Pep?'

'He was a bastard, Jed. He deserved what he got, but not from Emma. He deserved it from me and the children, and all the other people he bashed up and bullied.'

'He beat you too?'

'Oh, yes. Pep was a violent, nasty man. First we'd get the rages, the storm, the beatings. Then we'd get the sorries, the remorse, the presents and the soft soap. It would all be fine, for a bit, and then a few weeks later it would start again.'

'Did you do anything about it?' Jed asked. 'Did you tell anyone?'

'In those days, people weren't as big on listening as they are now. I took the kids and ran away. Rented a little flat in South Gosforth. Got the kids into a nice little school, right at the bottom of the street, and they settled really quickly. They loved it. I met Bob, and life was starting to look all right again. Then Pep managed to trace us, through the kids' school.'

'He came after you?'

She nodded. 'Stalking, I think they call it now. He'd just . . . follow me around, threaten me. He told me he was going to kill Bob. Told me he was going to take the kids. Told me he was going to arrange a little accident for me, when I was least expecting it. I was a basket case at the finish. It got so bad I was terrified to leave the house or cross the street. Bob got beaten senseless one night, ended up in hospital. I was suicidal. Then it suddenly stopped one day, just like that. Your sister turned out to be my salvation.'

'Emma?'

'Pep had found someone else, you see. We got divorced and life returned to what passes for normal up here. Then I heard about the wedding plans. I didn't know what to do, whether to go and see Emma and talk to her, tell her. Or do nothing, keep quiet in the hope that it would all fade away, like a bad memory. I mean, I didn't know – maybe Pep had changed. Maybe Emma was stronger than me.'

'So you didn't say anything?'

She shook her head, ashamed of herself. 'Bob

kept telling me that I should go and talk to Emma.
In the end, I told him I had, but I hadn't. I was
scared, you see. I thought that if Emma left Pep,
then he might turn on us again. I know I should
have done it. I should have warned her. I pray to
God that I'm forgiven.'

'Would you be willing to stand up in court and
tell them what you've just told me?'

'I don't know if I could, Jed.' He could see real
fear in her eyes.

'You ignored it once, and look what happened,'
Jed said. 'If you walk away from this again, Emma
could go to prison for a long, long time. She's got
a daughter, five years old, Beckie.' He kept piling
it on. 'She needs all the help she can get, Mary.
She needs *your* help.'

He looked hard into her eyes. She dropped
them to the floor and appeared to be thinking,
maybe agonising, even.

'I'll say what I know,' she said eventually.

'Thanks Mary.' He climbed off his stool and
gave her a hug.

'This is a major complication,' the young lawyer
complained to Jed, who had decided to pass on
the new development in his sister's case.

'But good news for the defence, yes?' Jed persisted.

'A not-guilty plea will mean a trial by jury,'
Fawdington sighed. 'A guilty plea means a simple
hearing and sentencing. It'll be time-consuming,
expensive, long and drawn out . . .'

'Can I ask a question?' Jed interrupted. 'Why

did a spineless little shit like you ever become a lawyer in the first place?'

'Well, frankly, it wasn't in order to end up defending the likes of your sister,' Fawdington retaliated.

'The likes of my sister?' Jed tapped him in the mouth, but it was a tap that sent the solicitor crashing to the floor.

'You fool!' the lawyer screamed. 'You stupid fool. I'll see that you're charged for this!'

'For what?' Jed smiled. 'Got any witnesses?'

Jed's next stop was Durham Jail, where he brought Emma up to date while a female prison officer hovered in the background. 'I don't want another solicitor, Jed,' Emma said when he had finished. 'What I did was wrong, so I'm gonna accept the punishment. An eye for an eye, like it says in the Bible.'

'But Emm . . .' Jed couldn't believe she was talking like that.

'But nowt. I did it, Jed. I took a life. It's not right. I deserve everything that comes my way.'

'And does Beckie deserve everything that comes *her* way? She deserves a life, Emma. She deserves to have her mum around when she's growing up. She deserves more than being dumped into council care.'

'You said you would look after her!'

'I didn't say I would *raise* her, Emma. That's not my job.'

'If you're trying to help me, Jed, you're not doing a very good job.'

'It's not about helping you,' he shouted, 'or about who's done what! It's about a little girl's future!' Emma put her hands over her eyes and he took a deep breath to compose himself. 'I'm sorry.'

'I miss her so much, Jed,' Emma sobbed.

'Look, Emma,' he tried again, 'I'm none too happy about what you did. But the dead are just that. Dead. Now it's time to look after the living.' There was no response so he tried a different tack. 'Maybe you're doing the right thing, hiding in here.'

'Hiding?'

'It'd be tough out there on the streets, people forever staring, pointing, whispering . . .'

'I know what you're trying to do, Jed. I'm not afraid of that.'

'Emma!' His temper flared again. 'We've got money, we've got barristers, we've got a credible witness, for God's sake! All we need is you. You've got to plead not guilty. If not for yourself, then for your daughter. The reason you wanted to marry Pep was to give Beckie the chance of a better life. This isn't it. So do it, Emma, do it!'

'All right,' she said, after a long pause.

'That's my girl.'

When the verdict on Emma came through as not guilty, the media went mad. Bowles and Connors watched the news that night in Bowles' apartment. They watched Jed descending the courtroom steps, chased by reporters, snappers and camera crews, and disappearing into a taxi.

Bowles switched the TV off with his remote, then, without warning, turned and punched Connors without breaking his stride, knocking him to the floor.

'Why did you do that?' Connors asked, struggling to his feet.

'Why didn't you kill Shepperd?' Bowles demanded.

'He was never on his own. I couldn't have made it look like an accident.'

'Forget accidents,' Bowles spat. 'Let's just have him dead. And don't screw up again.'

Connors nodded. 'It's either him or us.'

'No,' Bowles corrected him, 'it's either him or you.'

As Connors left the apartment, nursing a split lip, Bowles turned the television back on. Jed was still on the news. Bowles picked up a heavy metal ornament and hurled it at the screen, exploding five thousand pounds' worth of widescreen, Bang & Olufson technology.

CHAPTER TWENTY-ONE

'Jed! Jed Shepperd!' Quimby's all-too-familiar voice made Jed turn angrily as the reporter came into the recording studio with an envelope in his hand.

'The last time you came at me you ended up with a face full of fish,' Jed snarled. 'Now be warned.'

'Can't keep a good man down, Jed,' Quimby said cheerfully. 'Can I have a word?'

'I could stretch to two, no problem.'

'Droll, Jed, very droll.' Quimby obviously wasn't offended, and wasn't going away either. 'Last time we spoke, you got me thinking. Got my old creative juices flowing once again.'

'Really?' Jed was totally uninterested.

'Yeah, really. I started looking into a few things, things to do with your recent past. Did you know that the German police have reopened their investigation into Roxanne Pallenberg's death?'

'No.' Jed was surprised.

'No.' Quimby smiled. 'Nor, it seems, did the British police. You didn't know anything about that?'

Jed shook his head. 'How did you find out about that?'

'I talked to a policeman. At the Met.'

Jed looked suspicious. He was trying to work out Quimby's angle. 'Why?'

'Why what?'

'Why did you go to the trouble of finding out about all of this? What's in it for you?'

'There's a bigger story in this, Jed. I tried to forget about all that stuff you told me, about your manager being topped and you being framed, but I couldn't. It kept on going around and around, in here' – he tapped his temple – 'almost demanding me to look at it some more. So I did. But I can't get any further without your help.' Jed looked at him sceptically. 'I'm levelling with you, Jed. It's your call.'

Jed thought for a moment and then, against his better judgement, decided to take a punt. 'I gave the police a cassette,' he said, 'with a voice on it. Someone threatening Adrian, and they did nothing at all about it.'

'A Detective Inspector McClusky, was it?'

'Yeah.' Jed was shocked. 'How did—'

'You'd be surprised the folk you meet in the gutter, Jed. Leave it with me,' Quimby turned to go. 'Oh, Matt, my smudge, sent you these.' He handed him the envelope. 'Piccies of your concert. If you use any of 'em, bung him a few quid.'

As Quimby walked off Jed opened the envelope and pulled out the pictures. The first thing he saw was himself on stage. They were good strong images. Then he noticed someone fiddling in the background with some wires.

*   *   *

When Alan Clarke received a call from Paradigm asking him to go in to see Andy Morton he was puzzled. He took Lucy with him and the two of them were shown into Morton's office, a warm, welcoming room, not unlike the young man himself.

'It was a bit of a surprise, your call, out of the blue,' Alan admitted, 'I thought Dick Pilsbury would have torn up my telephone number, what with me striking out on my own.'

'Pilsbury's gone,' Morton said.

'He's gone?' Now Clarke was even more surprised, unsure of what was about to happen. His mind raced over all the possible consequences of this bit of news. 'I had a verbal agreement with Pilsbury regarding Paradigm Records releasing Jed Shepperd from his contract. If you've called me in here to tell me that agreement is now null and void—'

'I haven't,' Morton assured him.

'No?'

'There's been a lot of things happening in here that shouldn't have been. That's why we said goodbye to Pilsbury – and others.'

'Exactly what's been happening? As Jed's management representatives we have a right to be told.'

'I can't really go into detail right now,' Morton said, 'because of pending legal actions, but I can tell you that Jed, along with some of our other acts, was the victim of a scam involving Pilsbury and Warren Bowles.'

'Warren?' Now it was Lucy's turn to be shocked.

'What kind of scam?' Clarke asked.

'Cut-outs,' Morton said.

'Cut-outs?' Clarke let the news sink in then turned to Lucy. 'This isn't good, Lucy.' She looked confused and uncomfortable, unsure what role she might have played in whatever games Bowles had been orchestrating.

'We'll keep you fully informed of any developments,' Morton assured them. 'But I'd appreciate your cooperation in keeping this quiet, for now. There are other artists involved, and we'd like them to stay with us. We don't want to start a stampede.' Morton paused for a moment, aware that he was placing himself completely in Clarke's hands. Clarke did not break the silence and Morton continued. 'We don't know enough yet to start pointing the big finger, and we may well find so much that we don't want to point the finger at all. We may just have to get this settled quietly.'

'Okay,' Clarke agreed, 'we'll keep a lid on it, for now.'

Morton nodded his gratitude. 'I think we're going to owe Jed an awful lot of money.'

Lucy did not say a word until they were outside the building and walking back to Clarke's car. 'Warren Bowles stealing money from Jed?' she said eventually. 'I can't believe it.'

'There's worse, Lucy. If it is a cut-out scam, it can only work with the involvement of management.'

'Adrian?' Lucy was stunned. 'No!'

'Yeah. Let me talk to Jed.'

Lucy nodded, steadying herself from the shock on the car door, unable to speak.

Once Quimby started on somebody's case he was nothing if not persistent, as McClusky discovered when he came out of his house and walked over to his garage.

'Detective Inspector McClusky?' Quimby asked.

'Who are you?'

'Ted Quimby. I'm a journalist.' Quimby said. 'We're about to run a story on Adrian Lynn, Jed Shepperd's ex-manager, who was found in the Thames. Would you like to comment on why that investigation came to a halt?'

'No comment.' McClusky's anger seemed edged with panic. 'Who gave you this address?'

Quimby ignored the question and ploughed on. 'Would you like to comment on Jed Shepperd's allegations that he was framed – that he was stitched up and wrongly put in prison?'

'No comment.' McClusky looked uncomfortable and Quimby knew that he was onto something.

'Would you like to comment on the death of Shepperd's former personal assistant, Roxanne Pallenberg, who was found dead in her Hamburg apartment, as a result of a suspected overdose of barbiturates?'

'No comment.' McClusky seemed to have sweat breaking out from every pore. He obviously wasn't used to being treated like this. He made for his car but Quimby kept talking.

'Would you like to comment on the fact that the

German police have now reopened that investigation and are treating her death as suspicious?'

'No comment.' McClusky opened his car door but there wasn't much room as he tried to squeeze through the gap.

'Would you like to comment on a tape recording that was allegedly given to you by Jed Shepperd and may have identified the murderer of Adrian Lynn?'

'No comment.' He managed to get into the car and close the door but Quimby was still shouting through the window.

'Would you like to comment on the fact that you have no comment?'

'No comment!' McClusky shouted, almost running over the reporter as he sped out of the garage.

Once he'd left Quimby a safe distance behind, McClusky dialled his car phone. 'It's McClusky here,' he said. 'I've just had the press all over me regarding Jed Shepperd. They seem to know quite a lot. We're gonna have to do something quickly.'

The day after the meeting at Paradigm, Clarke met Jed in Newcastle. Clarke suggested that they should take a walk along the quayside under the Tyne Bridge while he tried to explain what was happening.

'What is a cut-out, then?' Jed asked eventually. 'It's not something they do with cornflake boxes on *Blue Peter*, I take it?'

'You take a record that's already selling,' Clarke

said, 'and you delete it. Cut a little hole out of
the cover – hence "cut-out". You then sell all the
stock on to a company that specialises in buying
up deletions. That company in turn sells the stock
on as current, and so charges the going rate for it.'

Jed tried to take it in. 'How do you delete a
record that's still selling?'

'If the computer logs a record selling less than
ten copies over two consecutive accounting peri-
ods, it automatically marks it for deletion.'

'But my records were still selling,' Jed protested.

'The computer just does what you tell it to.'

'But to get that to work, they'd *all* have to be
mixed up in this?'

Clarke nodded. 'Pilsbury designated your product, and that of some of the other Paradigm acts,
as deleted. And the deletions company he was
selling to was owned by him and Warren Bowles
and—'

'Bowles,' Jed exclaimed. 'I knew from the off
that he was a wrong un.' He thought for a second.
'Poor Lucy.'

'. . . And someone else,' Clarke said cautiously.

'Yeah?'

'There's no proof, as yet, so it's not definite.'
Clarke plucked up his courage. 'But the management would have to know about it.'

'Adrian?' Jed was stunned. 'No!'

'For this kind of scam to work, the manager
would have to be a co-director of the deletions
company, along with Pilsbury and Bowles in
this case.'

Jed shook his head sadly. 'Does Lucy know?'

'She's beside herself,' Clarke said, 'absolutely gutted, and if you don't want her around any more she'll totally understand. Might be easier all round.'

'No. Let's concentrate on getting to the bottom of all this. We still don't know what happened to Adrian, and, whether he ripped me off or not, I'm gonna find out. I owe him that much.'

'You're a better man than I am, Gunga Din,' Clarke said admiringly. 'There is some good news. According to Morton, Paradigm owe you a lot of money.'

'A lot?'

'A lot!' Clarke nodded. 'Now I've learned the hard way never to get excited about bread until it's actually in the bank. However on this occasion I've decided to throw caution to the wind.' He grinned and led Jed over to a motorcycle parked under a green tarpaulin. Alan pulled off the cover with a flourish to reveal a gleaming new, bottle-green Triumph 900 with two helmets on the ground beside it.

'Oh, man!' Jed was impressed.

'Hope it's the right one.'

'Same as the old one. Oh, boy!' He climbed onto the bike and started it up, the throaty metal roar making him smile.

'I would've preferred to be giving you a hefty advance,' Alan shouted over the din of the engine, 'but I just can't afford it right now.'

'This'll do fine for the moment,' Jed said. 'You wanna come and hear what you're buying into?'

'Yes please!' They both pulled on the helmets and Jed slid them out into the traffic.

As McClusky walked from his car to Warren Bowles' front door he noticed that the road diggers were sitting around in their tent, brewing up yet again. Everything was making him nervous and when he reached the apartment he was unable to sit down, pacing around the floor as he recounted his run-in with Quimby. Bowles sat back, nursing a tumbler full of whisky and enjoying the policeman's discomfort.

'There's nothing to worry about,' Bowles said patronisingly. 'It's all been taken care of.'

'You reckon?' McClusky sounded doubtful.

'I know,' Bowles assured him. 'Jed Shepperd is history. But you didn't hear it from me, officer.'

'You've not . . . ?'

'Not yet.' Bowles checked his watch. 'But, even as we speak—'

'Connors?' McClusky asked. 'That good for nothing—'

'No,' Bowles interrupted. 'He's good for something. He's good at one particular thing.'

'You shouldn't have—'

'*We* shouldn't have.' Bowles cut him short. 'When are you going to get the hang of it? It's we. *We*! We're in this together.' McClusky shook his head and Bowles seemed to relax. 'It's good for pop stars to die young. Saves them drying up and becoming minicab drivers.'

CHAPTER TWENTY-TWO

Clarke sat next to Jed in the recording studio, listening to an almost finished version of 'Country Boy'. Jed waited nervously for his verdict.

'Oh, yes,' Alan said when it finally came to an end. 'That'll do. Are there any more like this?'

'Seven or eight new songs,' Jed admitted. 'Been coming thick and fast ever since I played the benefit gig. No stopping it. I really feel like it's coming back.'

'Can you run me a cassette of that off?' Clarke asked, getting up to go.

'Sure. Where are you going?'

'There's a lot to do, Jed. We've had some producers sniffing about for a live TV. I wasn't sure if you'd be ready, but after listening to that, there's no doubt. That's your single.'

'Isn't it a bit early for a telly?'

'You're not nervous, are you?'

'I'm not nervous. I'm ready. But you know what they'll wanna talk about.'

'This one's the biggest TV audience in the country,' Alan argued. 'It'll give us the platform we need. No better way to let the people know you're back.'

'Let me think about it, Alan.'

'Don't take too long,' Clarke warned. 'I'd like to get a record out a.s.a.p.' He picked up his cassette and headed for the door.

'Where's Lucy now?' Jed asked.

'In London, looking for Pilsbury.'

'If she has any joy, give me a call. I'd like to have a little chat with Mr Pilsbury.'

In his office at the police station, McClusky was playing Adrian's answering machine cassette to two of his superiors. When the threatening message finished McClusky switched it off and the three of them sat in silence.

'How long have you been sitting on that?' one of the senior officers asked eventually.

'Too long, sir,' McClusky answered and they fell once more into a troubled silence.

Jed used the new motorbike to tempt Wendy out with him for a cup of tea. They rode down to the nearby harbour and parked up by a tea stand. Jed bought a couple of plastic cups and they walked a few feet above the water.

'Tea by the sea and a new toy,' Wendy remarked. 'What are you celebrating? It must be something big.'

'Alan gave me the bike as a signing-on gift,' Jed told her. 'And we're close to finding out what happened to Adrian. I can finally see some light at the end of the tunnel.'

'I'm glad for you, Jed,' she said. 'You were dealt a really shit hand. It's about time you had a break.'

'Can you remember when we were arguing in your kitchen and you said to me you loved me?' Jed asked.

'What I actually said,' Wendy corrected him, 'was that as I got to know you better, I loved you more but I liked you less.'

'Did you mean it?'

'Yes.' Jed stopped in his tracks and dropped to one knee. 'What are you doing?'

He pulled a small box from his pocket and opened it up, taking out a huge diamond ring. 'Will you marry me?'

The fishermen who were mending their nets nearby stopped to watch the show.

'Jed, man,' she laughed, 'I'm embarrassed. Get up.'

'Not until you give me an answer.'

She tried to ignore their audience. 'Where do you stand with Lucy, Jed?'

'She's Adrian's sister. No more. I swear it. I love you, Wendy.'

She looked into his eyes for a moment and took a deep breath. 'All right, yes, I will. Now would you get up off the ground, please?'

He stood up and kissed her. 'I know I've not always been Mr Perfect . . .'

'This is true. In fact you've regularly been a complete and utter shit.'

'I know.'

'But I forgive you.' They kissed again.

'One thing, though,' Jed said. 'A very important prenuptial agreement point. You're gonna have to get rid of all those old records of yours.

Can't have you listening to anyone else but me, all right?'

Wendy gave him a playful push backwards, but he stumbled, lost his balance for a moment and seemed to hover in mid-air. Then he plunged into the sea.

At the next meeting in McClusky's office several other senior officers were also present, some of them from police forces in other countries. McClusky played the tape again and they all listened, their faces grave. At the end of the tape McClusky's superior switched the machine off. 'That's put the cat among the pigeons,' he said to the room in general.

'You say the press now know about this?' another one asked McClusky.

'Yes, sir,' McClusky said, his face showing no emotion. There was a murmur of disquiet around the room. 'What do you want me to do, sir?'

'Sit tight,' his boss instructed. 'We'll let you know, when we know.'

When Jed and Wendy got back to Wendy's house the message light on the answerphone was blinking.

'You'd better plodge through to the bathroom,' Wendy told a very wet Jed, 'and take a shower.'

'I might need some help getting all this nasty wet kit off,' Jed teased.

Wendy grinned naughtily. 'This might be your lucky day.'

'Yee-haw!' Jed whooped and pointed to the

phone. 'You've got a message there, wifey! Better not be some sneaky boyfriend.' As he disappeared into the bathroom Wendy pressed the play button. 'Wedding Bells For The Geordie Lad,' Jed shouted back. 'I can see the headline now!'

Lucy's voice came out of the machine. 'Jed, it's Lucy. Could you call me on my home number? It's very important. Thanks my love. Bye.'

Wendy shook her head. 'I don't believe it!'

Jed heard the slamming of the front door and came back into the sitting room. 'Wendy?' Realising she had gone, he played the message back. The moment it finished he dialled Lucy's number.

'Lucy?'

'Jed,' Lucy replied. 'I've found Pilsbury. He's holed up on a houseboat on the Thames.'

Wendy slammed the door of the house. She was furious – furious and confused. The . . . the utter cheek of the man. How could he, after all he had said? After giving her the ring? After calling her wifey, for God's sake?

As she stepped onto the pavement she saw a man stooped down next to Jed's Triumph. He seemed to be fiddling with the back wheel.

'Hoy,' she yelled. 'What are you doing?'

'Just admiring the machine.' The man stood up and smiled. 'You don't see many of them about.'

'Well, just leave it alone and bugger off,' Wendy snapped.

'Of course.' The man disappeared and Wendy

237

looked back towards her house. In the picture window she could see Jed deep in conversation on the phone, nodding and jotting something down.

Her disappointment made her feel even angrier.

Omo and Big Chrissie were working away, packing panties into envelopes and scribbling handwritten notes, apparently drowning in orders, when Omo suddenly looked at his watch, stood up and put his coat on.

'Where are you going?' Chrissie asked.

'I've got to go . . .' Omo hedged, 'to me auntie's.'

'What, now?' Chrissie was aghast. 'We're stowed off, man! Who's gonna lick the envelopes?'

'I promised,' Omo said, going out. Chrissie grabbed his coat and followed, his suspicions aroused.

Omo made his way through the streets to the church. Inside, the church was empty. Omo wandered around like a lost soul. He noticed the silver on the altar and went over for a closer look.

'Hello,' a voice said suddenly, making him jump back in fright, his fists raised in defence.

'Oops.' He saw that it was Kate – and dropped his dukes. 'Sorry. I'm sorry I'm late. Pressure of work. That's what happens when you run your own show.'

'You poor thing,' Kate sympathised. 'What kind of business are you in, Norman?'

Omo winced at the mention of his hated formal name. 'Mail-order,' he said quickly.

'Oh.' Kate could see that he didn't want to elaborate. 'Well, it's lovely to see you.'

'It's lovely to see you an' all,' Omo assured her. 'I'd like to see a bit more, like. If you know what I mean.'

'Would you like a cup of tea?' Kate asked kindly.

'Tea?' He looked as if she had asked him to drink effluent.

'Yes.'

'Go on then.' She led the way and he followed, chatting nervously. 'Eeh! Last time I was in one of these places I was hoisting the lead off the roof.'

'Hoisting?' Kate was puzzled.

'Aye, er . . .' Omo back-pedalled. 'Hoisting it up into the air, like. So's it could be replaced, with new stuff.'

'Oh, I see. I thought you meant you were stealing it, for one awful moment.' He could see that she knew very well what he had meant.

'Listen,' he said, 'you won't tell anyone about this, will you?'

'A cup of tea?'

'Me coming into a church. Me life wouldn't be worth living if me mates got wind of it.'

'It'll be our little secret.' She smiled. 'Just you, and me and' – she pointed upwards – 'Him.'

'Who?' Omo asked suspiciously. 'Oh, aye, the big man.'

In London, Dick Pilsbury returned to his handsome, ocean-going boat, his arms full of shopping. When he went into the living area, he

239

jumped back as he saw two people waiting for him. 'Jesus! You nearly gave me a heart attack.'

'That would've been getting off too lightly, pal,' Jed told him. Lucy was sitting with him.

'I know what you must think, Jed.' Pilsbury tried to reason with them. 'But the decision to shaft you wasn't down to me.'

'I'm not here to talk about me,' Jed said. 'I want to know what happened to Adrian.'

'I had nothing to do with it.'

'With what, exactly?'

'You should talk to Warren about it.' Lucy turned and walked out of the room. Jed let her go.

'I'm here to talk to you,' he told Pilsbury, 'and I'll be getting some answers, believe me.' Pilsbury shrugged, apparently unthreatened. Then Lucy came back in carrying a can of petrol. Without a word she began splashing it around the living room, slopping a bit onto Pilsbury as she passed him. Jed was almost as shocked as Pilsbury.

'Er, Lucy,' he said, tentatively.

'What're you doing?' Pilsbury demanded.

'I'm sick of all this talk,' Lucy told him. 'My brother's dead!' She continued dousing the place with petrol.

'Don't do that,' Pilsbury was beginning to panic, 'I'll tell you everything, anything you want to know, but I honestly don't think you're going to want to hear it.'

'Go to hell!' Lucy snapped.

'We need to hear it from somebody, Lucy,' Jed interjected.

Lucy stopped, looked at Jed and then at Pilsbury. 'I'll give you one minute,' she announced.

'One minute?' She didn't move. 'Okay, okay. You know about the cut-out scam.'

'We know,' Jed told him.

'And that Adrian was running it? That it was his idea?'

'I'll burn you alive, you bastard,' Lucy threatened.

'I told you you wouldn't want to hear it,' Pilsbury shouted, 'but it's the truth. If it's any consolation, you weren't the only one. We were creaming off a dozen big acts. Then suddenly, Adrian wasn't paying Bowles his slice. Don't ask me why. He was asked and asked, and then Bowles got sick of asking and sent Connors down one day. The next thing I knew your brother was dead.'

Lucy sat down, near to tears and both men heaved a sigh of relief. She lashed out at the petrol can and smashed her fist down onto the table.

'Where does this leave me?' Pilsbury asked.

'Shipwrecked, pal,' Lucy told him.

As she and Jed got back to the embankment, Jed could see she was still very upset. 'Are you all right?'

'I'm just angry. I'm angry with Adrian, because I know it's true.' She looked at Jed. 'What now?'

'I'm gonna see Warren Bowles.'

241

'I've already tried that. He's not there, out of town for the day. I haven't had a chance to apologise, Jed, for—'

Jed shook his head. 'Adrian was Adrian was Adrian. You're not your brother, Lucy.'

'No, I wanted to apologise for calling you at Wendy's. I never thought—'

'Never mind.' Jed shrugged. 'What's a wedding?'

The full horror hit Lucy. 'Oh, shit.'

They walked on for a few moments in silence. 'You wouldn't have, would you?' Jed asked.

'What?'

'Torched the boat?'

'Oh yes. Whatever else he was, Adrian was my brother.'

When Omo emerged from the church Big Chrissie was still waiting for him. As Omo passed in the darkened street Chrissie reached out and pulled him into the doorway. 'What have you been doing?' he demanded.

'Nothing.'

'Have you been using that place as a meet to set up your own deals?'

'There was nabody in there!' Omo protested.

'You're not thinking of going solo, are you?'

'Hadaway, man. I wouldn't do that.'

'What were you doing, then? You'll be telling me you were trying to pull the vicar.'

Omo gulped, considered telling the truth, and then decided Chrissie wouldn't believe him anyway. 'I was prayin'.'

'Praying?' Chrissie was gobsmacked. 'You're never a God-botherer?'

'Praying for business to pick up. Owt's worth a try, eh?'

CHAPTER TWENTY-THREE

Wendy stood outside her front door and stared at the piles of flowers awaiting her return. She stooped down to read a handwritten card taped to the largest bouquet. It simply said, 'I love you'. She kicked the flowers out of the way and went inside.

Feeling confused and profoundly unhappy, she contemplated an evening alone. As she weighed up her options, deciding that now wasn't the right time to make decisions, the doorbell rang urgently. She ignored it. It rang again – and again.

'Wendy? I know you're in there.' Jed's voice pleaded. 'Please answer the door, Wendy. It's important.'

Wendy sat it out, half wanting to let him in, but the more stubborn stronger part wanting him to go to hell.

Outside, Jed gave up shouting and stood, wondering what to do. The elderly woman from next door appeared from the back of the house carrying a bucket of water. Jed prepared himself to smile and be civil but she launched the contents of the bucket over him. 'You're a bloody disgrace,' she shouted and walked away, leaving Jed soaked and

245

speechless. Deciding he was beaten, he made his way back to his bike and rode off.

Connors pulled away in his car and fell in behind the bike, far enough not to attract Jed's attention. Once they were out on the main road Connors pressed the accelerator and started to close the gap. Jed took a turning and passed through some bollards that restricted passage to bikers only.

All Connors could do was watch the bike disappearing into the distance.

Archie was working happily at the lathe in his shed when two men quietly let themselves in.

'Mr Tate?' the first one asked.

'Thanks son,' Archie said, not looking up from his work. 'Just leave them in the usual place, there.'

'Mr Tate!' the man repeated. Archie turned impatiently and the man held up some ID. 'I'm from the DSS.'

Archie looked at them for a moment, realised the game was up and smiled. 'Can I make you a cup of tea?' he asked. 'I was just about to put the kettle on.'

'That's very good of you, under the circumstances,' the man replied.

'We've all got a job to do, eh?' Archie picked up the kettle and made for the door. 'Not be a minute.' The moment he was outside Archie shut the door and bolted it, chucking the kettle and running for his life across the allotment.

* * *

Wendy was lying awake in bed when the buzzer went again. She smiled and slowly made her way downstairs. She felt ready to talk to him now, but didn't intend to give him an easy time of it.

'Jed!' she shouted through the door. 'It's the middle of the night, for God's sake! But . . .' She threw open the door and her smile faded as she saw a man standing on the doorstep. She thought she recognised him.

'Hello,' he said.

'You're the bugger that was messing around with Jed's bike, aren't you?'

Before she could say anything else he pushed her back into the hallway and slammed the door behind him. She went to scream but he grabbed her throat, squeezing her into silence. 'You'd best behave yourself, darling. I like squeezing people's necks.' He tightened his grip. 'Sometimes, I don't know when to stop.'

He forced her to sit down and sat with her, waiting. Just then the phone rang and the answering machine cut in. Jed's voice came over the line. 'Hi, Wendy. It's Jed. I want to explain everything, and I would, if I could. But I've got to do this telly thing in London. Please watch the show tomorrow night if you can. I'm sure you'll understand when you see it.'

Wendy wanted to reach out to the phone and talk to him so much that she started to cry.

'I love you,' Jed said and hung up.

'Ahhh,' her attacker mocked. 'Isn't that sweet! So he's not coming back? All right, on your feet.' Wendy stood up, terrified of what might be coming.

In London the next morning Jed made his way to Bowles' apartment, passing the road-diggers' tent on the way and noticing they were sitting around drinking tea as usual. Bowles opened the door himself. 'Jed. What a wonderful surprise.'

'Oh.' Jed pushed past. 'I've got more.'

'Really?' Bowles could see there was nothing he could do to stop him.

Jed took in the sumptuous apartment. 'Well, well, Warren,' he said, 'you're a star and no mistake.'

Bowles sat down in a large armchair flanked by two huge stone Buddhas. 'Surely you're the star, Jed,' he said calmly, 'albeit a star on the wane.'

'I saw Mr Pilsbury the other day. He had quite a lot to say about you. About your involvement in Adrian's death, and my financial ruin.'

'He said that?' Bowles mocked surprise. 'Ooh.'

'You can act as cool as you want, Warren, but you've got dirty hands and I'm gonna nail your arse to the wall.'

'Very descriptive, Jed. But it's not on the cards.'

'Isn't it? I've got Pilsbury, and a tape recording that'll put you away for a long time.'

Bowles didn't answer for a few moments. 'What do you want me to say, Jed? I'm scared? Is that what you want to hear?' His smile faded, leaving only a cold ruthlessness. 'Let Pilsbury stand up in court. I'll stand there with my hundred-grand lawyers and we'll see what happens. You're out of your depth, Jed. This is no place for a dumb Northern working-class dickhead. You should have just stayed where you were, strumming your stupid guitar up there in shipyard-land. So why don't you be a good lad and go back to where you belong.'

Jed shook his head, surprisingly calmly. 'That's always been my trouble,' he said. 'I've never known my place.'

'Smart words, Jed. But if there's nothing else, it's time for you to leave.'

'I gave you a chance,' Jed said, 'which is more than you gave Adrian, or Roxanne, or me. Enjoy the programme tonight.'

He walked out, leaving Bowles wondering what he was up to.

In the Legion Club, Archie was keeping a low profile, miserably nursing a pint.

'Captured by the social, eh?' Bobby said smugly.

'Not captured,' Archie said proudly. 'I managed to escape, but the game's up.'

'If you're on the dole you shouldn't be getting your hands dirty fiddlin',' Bobby said pompously. 'I've nae sympathy.'

One of the elderly committee men approached Bobby. 'Can I have a word, son?'

'I'm a bit busy at the minute, Cyril.' Bobby tried to shoo him away so he could enjoy Archie's misery a bit longer. 'Is it important?'

'There seems to be a discrepancy with your medals,' the old man said.

The colour drained from Bobby's face. 'Really?'

'The Africa Star.' Cyril pointed. 'It's from the Second World War. You're wearing it next to your Falkland DSM, there.' Bobby looked down at the medals and Archie felt himself cheering up. 'The committee would like to see you at oh nine hundred hours tomorrow.'

'Right,' Bobby said, resigned to the fact that his game too was now up.

As Jed played 'Country Boy' on the television, a number of people with vested interests were watching. All the lads except Omo were watching at the Legion, while Emma and Beckie watched proudly at home. A group of senior policemen, including McClusky, had their eyes fixed intently on the screen at the police station and Bowles sat in his apartment trying to work out why Jed had warned him to watch. Behind the scenes at Television Centre, Clarke and Lucy were watching on a monitor in the green room. As Jed finished his song and took off his guitar the audience roared their approval. He made his way over to the show's host, who was sitting in one of two big chairs. The show's host rose to greet him and they both sat down.

'Jed Shepperd, ladies and gentlemen!' the host announced to the audience before turning to his guest. 'Thanks for coming, Jed. Great to have you back on the show.'

'Great to be here,' Jed responded. 'Thanks for having me.'

'So, Jed, it's been a while since we've heard anything from you. But not *about* you, of course!

You've had your share of ups and downs, haven't you?'

'You could say that.'

'The death of your manager, then a drug bust, and then jail! How did you manage to keep going?'

'Faith,' Jed said, 'faith in the truth. Adrian Lynn, my manager and my friend, was killed for no apparent reason. We did the right thing. We went to the police, talked to a Detective Inspector McClusky, but they did nothing.'

'Well,' the host suggested hastily, 'maybe they had nothing to go on.'

'Oh, yes they did,' Jed insisted. 'There's always been a substantial piece of evidence that's been totally ignored.'

The chat-show host, unused to controversy on the air, was beginning to sweat and glanced off set towards his producer for guidance. 'Really?' he said.

'I'd like you all to listen to something,' Jed said to the camera. He pulled out a small tape recorder and held it to the microphone.

'Nothing offensive, I hope.' The host was now very jittery indeed. 'We are going out live, you know!'

Jed nodded. 'There's a voice on this tape. I don't know who it is, but if I can put a name to it, I can maybe solve a riddle that the police haven't managed, or wanted, to solve.' He pulled out the picture of Connors fiddling backstage with the wires at Emma's benefit and held it up to the camera. 'Does the voice belong to this man? This face? Somebody help me, please!'

The studio had fallen absolutely silent as Jed hit the play button on the machine and a male voice came clearly through: '. . . Adrian, what the hell's going on? You promised me the transfer would go through on Monday and nothing has turned up . . . made me look a right fool, you have . . . I don't think you realise how serious this is . . . they're not happy at this end, the boss is going apeshit . . . threatening all kinds of things . . . you know what'll happen if you default once more . . .'

At the police station, McClusky and his superiors were already leaving the room before the message had finished playing, as if a decision had now been made for them and all they had to do was act on it.

In the Legion Club the lads watched, mystified by whatever Jed was up to.

Bowles knew exactly what he was up to.

And at the vicarage, Omo couldn't have cared less, since he and Kate had fallen into a passionate clinch on the sofa during Jed's song and were both now completely unaware of what was happening on screen.

Bowles was hastily packing a bag when the doorbell went and Connors stood on the step, grinning. 'Guess who's coming to dinner,' he said, pulling Wendy inside. Her hands were tied and she had a handkerchief in her mouth. Her eyes were wide with terror.

'Who the hell is this?' Bowles couldn't believe what he saw.

'Only Jed Shepperd's fiancée.' Connors beamed. He was very pleased with himself.

'Why have you brought her here?'

'Think about it. We just have to let him know where we are and who we've got here with us. He'll come running. Then I can kill him.'

'Have you lost your mind?' Bowles shouted. 'Why would we want to bring Shepperd and the rest of the world here, to my door?'

'I thought you'd be pleased.' Connors seemed hurt by his boss's disapproval.

'Pleased? You moron. You bring this . . . bimbo—'

'Don't call me a fucking bimbo,' she spluttered from behind the gag.

'You bring her here, in full view of the Metropolitan Police.'

'There aren't any cops around.' Connors was puzzled by this reaction. 'I checked.'

'You checked? Didn't you see the road-diggers outside?'

'Yeah. They've been there for ages.'

'That's right, shit-for-brains . . .'

'What's going on?' Connors was now totally mystified.

'Right,' Bowles said, trying to take stock of the situation, 'bring her along. We're going up to Elstree.'

'But if the Old Bill's outside they're gonna see her,' Connors reasoned.

'Yes, and then we'll get left alone. They'll not want to start shooting at us while she's in the way.'

Bowles hustled them both out of the apartment and down to the car.

In the green room, once the show was over, the producer read Jed the riot act. Alan Clarke could do nothing but stand by and look sheepish. 'This is an entertainment show,' the producer yelled, 'not a soapbox for personal grievances.'

'I'm sorry,' Clarke said, turning to Jed, 'aren't we?'

'It's a talk show,' Jed said. 'I was talking.'

'You were supposed to be plugging!' the producer fumed. 'That's the game and you know it! Not airing all your dirty laundry or playing Inspector Bloody Clouseau!'

'I'm sorry,' Jed said, 'but it was my only chance.'

'Well, you just blew it, sunshine,' the producer said. 'Big time!'

As the producer flounced off McClusky appeared with another man, whose bearing told Jed that he was the DI's superior. He confirmed this by taking command of the situation. Jed was startled to have got such a quick result.

'Mr Shepperd,' the senior officer said, 'would you mind coming with us, please?'

'What have I done now?' Jed asked.

'You've just totally ruined an eighteen-month undercover operation that involved police forces in seven other countries. And wasted a massive amount of police time and taxpayers' money!' the policeman told him.

'I was only trying to help,' Jed protested.

'You're arresting him?' Alan Clarke couldn't believe his eyes.

'He'll be helping us with our enquiries,' the man said, leading Jed away.

'I'm coming with you, Jed,' Lucy called out.

'No, you're not,' the policeman snapped, and as they left a stunned silence fell over the room. Clarke let his head sink into his hands.

Connors and Bowles took Wendy, still gagged and tied, to the underground car park in the lift and led her to a brand-new black Range Rover,

'I'm not going anywhere with you, you fucking maniacs!' she mumbled, almost inaudibly.

'Be quiet,' Bowles ordered, and Connors bundled her into the back seat. Connors got behind the wheel and Bowles climbed into the passenger seat. But as they started forward two men ran into their path, one pulling a gun.

'Halt!' the man shouted. 'Armed police!'

Connors gleefully stamped on the gas, making the men jump for safety as the Range Rover tore out of the garage, scattering other police, including the road-diggers, as it emerged into the night. In his rear-view mirror he saw that one man, knocked to the ground, had pulled out a radio and, he assumed, was calling for back-up.

Jed was squashed into the back of a police car between McClusky and his boss. 'We were so close to cracking all of this,' McClusky was saying, 'and you have to force our hand with your bloody TV theatrics.'

'Cracking what?' Jed asked.

'We've been after your friend Bowles for a long time,' the senior man explained

'He's no friend of mine!'

'Illegal financial transactions, money laundering, huge sums involved. The crossborder sale of narcotics. A whole host of unsavoury things. But he's been a clever boy, never got his own hands dirty, always covered his tracks.'

'But he made a mistake,' McClusky interrupted his boss, 'and the Serious Fraud boys found it. We were just about to move in on him for fraudulent financial practice when the bloody press moved in on me, about you!'

'Do you have anything to tie Bowles in to Adrian Lynn's death?' Jed asked.

'That's rather complicated,' the senior man said, hedging. At that moment the message came through on the car radio.

'Bowles is on the move in the Range Rover,' the voice came through the radio. 'He's got Connors with him and one other. Female. A hostage by the look of it. Connors arrived with her here a half hour ago.'

Jed felt a chilly sweat breaking out through his skin. Something deep inside told him who Bowles' hostage was, and it was going to make a big difference. 'What does she look like?' His voice seemed to be cracking under the pressure of trying to sound calm. 'The girl?'

McClusky looked at him and sensed that Jed knew something. 'Description of the female, please,' he said into the radio.

'Five-five,' the voice replied and Jed felt a sickening lurch in his stomach. 'Short dark hair, cut in a bob, wearing a yellow jacket and black leather trousers.'

'That's Wendy,' Jed heard himself say, 'my fiancée.' Suddenly everything had changed. Whereas before it had seemed like a highly dangerous game, now it felt deeply personal. He wanted to kill anyone who even frightened Wendy, let alone hurt her. He hadn't felt that strongly about anyone for many years, not since his wife and child had died, killed by a gas-fitter's carelessness. It was as if a long numbness had suddenly worn off, leaving an open wound behind.

McClusky took in the news and turned to his superior. 'My guess,' he said, 'is that he'll head up to Elstree. He's got the plane there. We have an excuse to pull him, if he's taken a hostage.'

Jed waited for the senior man to agree, but he was lost in thought. A few seconds ticked by, but it seemed like an eternity to Jed. Every moment they kept speeding down the road took him further from Wendy. 'What are you waiting for?' he exploded. 'Turn the bloody car around!'

The policeman was jolted into a decision. He nodded and the driver did a ferocious U-turn.

As the Range Rover hurtled up the A1, Warren Bowles' brain was racing. The adrenalin was pumping through his veins and he felt strangely exhilarated. His life had lacked this sort of excitement recently. It had all been getting too easy. He had been allowing himself to become flabby.

Now he was back on the front line, fighting for his life and freedom, a fox outwitting the dumb hounds.

'Pull up here,' he ordered Connors as they reached a secluded spot on the perimeter road of the aerodrome. The Lear jet was taxiing out of the hangar in readiness. All he had to do was find a way of getting into it alone. 'Get her out onto the road!' he said.

'Right!' Connors obeyed, like the good soldier he was. Wendy's eyes widened with fear above her gag. Was this going to be where they executed her and left her in a heap for the police to find? She punched and kicked at Connors as he pulled her out, but he was too strong for her. While he battled with Wendy, Bowles slid into the driver's seat and wound down the window.

'Not be long,' he said, pressing the accelerator to the floor and speeding away.

'Warren!' Connors shouted after him, trying to work out what Bowles was up to at the same time as controlling Wendy's thrashing limbs. 'Warren!'

As the police car drew up its occupants could just make out the shape of the Lear in the dark. If Jed had had a gun he would have used it to force the police driver to head straight for it, anything to stop Bowles from getting away with Wendy. He now realised that he never wanted to be without her. He had been on his own too long. He didn't want to go back to that now that he had found her.

'He can't take off in this,' McClusky's boss said, gesturing at the blackness all around. 'Can he?'

'He can in a Lear, sir,' McClusky replied, picking up the radio. 'McClusky here. Someone get onto Elstree Aerodrome and lock it down. Nothing to come in or out. Understand?'

'Copy,' a voice replied.

Jed felt a wave of relief as the car sped forward, joined by others, and pulled up in front of the plane. He leapt out with McClusky and the others and ran up the steps to the jet. Inside they found only a confused pilot. There was no sign of Bowles, Connors or Wendy. Jed felt like screaming. If Bowles wasn't there he could be anywhere. They had lost them. It could take hours to find the Range Rover again. They were going to have to wait until Bowles contacted them, or until Wendy's body turned up like Adrian's and Roxanne's. He made his way back down to the tarmac and stood around with the others, feeling desperate and afraid.

Now that Bowles had got rid of Connors he felt invincible. He felt he could outwit all of them. As he gunned the engine of the Range Rover and headed for the men on the tarmac his only intention was to wipe out as many as possible, fell them like bowling pins. If he could clear the runway the plane would be able to take off, with him in it. It was just a matter of brute force.

'Look out!' McClusky shouted as he spotted the car heading out of the blackness for them at full speed. The police scattered and Bowles shot through the middle. Slamming on the brakes, he threw the car into reverse and headed back, the blood pumping through his brain.

Jed, relieved to find that they hadn't lost Bowles after all, glanced at the chaos all around him. There were policemen running in all directions but none of them seemed to know what to do. If Bowles drove off into the night now he would get clean away. The only hope of saving Wendy lay in stopping the car now. Seeing the Range Rover coming back towards him, Jed leapt up the steps of the aircraft and climbed onto the wing. As the car went underneath he dived out onto the bonnet. The sight of Bowles' face through the windscreen made him furious. He wanted to kill the man for daring to lay hands on Wendy. Holding on for dear life, he punched at the glass. 'Where's my girl, you bastard?' he shouted.

For a moment Bowles was startled. He hadn't expected this. He had expected to be able to use the car as a weapon to disperse the enemy, but now one of them was on board, uncomfortably close. He had to shake Jed off before he did anything else, and he had to do it fast, before any of the police made it back to their cars. He floored the gas pedal and braked savagely in an attempt to throw him off.

Jed grabbed a windscreen wiper, but it came off in his hand, sending him sliding back down the bonnet. He grabbed at the ventilator slats, his fingers screaming out with pain as he hung on for his life.

The vehicle swerved madly from side to side.

Bowles seemed determined to get rid of him. Eventually, Jed felt his grip weaken and he was thrown off the bonnet into the darkness, landing with a painful thump on the tarmac.

Bowles checked in his rear-view mirror, trying to see where Jed had fallen so that he could finish him off. He recognised that Jed was the biggest danger to him. There was no sign of him getting up. 'One down . . .' he said aloud, and he grinned. He turned his attention back to the windscreen, just in time to see the fuel tanker parked up ahead, but not in time to hit the brakes. The car smashed into the tanker side on and the explosion lit the aerodrome, frying Warren Bowles to a crisp in the process.

As Jed pulled himself painfully to his feet, he saw Connors being pushed into one of the cars by two policemen. And there was Wendy, standing, looking at him across the tarmac. He stumbled towards her and she made a few shaky steps in his direction. The tanker was still burning as they fell into each other's arms, both hanging on to keep themselves from collapsing. Neither could find the words to express themselves, but each knew what the other was feeling. Neither wanted to be separated from the other ever again.

As the police drove them back to London Jed just wanted to put an end to the whole episode and head back up north. He wanted to start afresh with Wendy and to forget everything else that had happened.

'There's one person I want to see before we go

home,' he told her once they were on their own. 'Come with me?'

She nodded, willing to trust him, knowing now just how strong his feelings were for her, confident they were going to be together. He drove her to the cemetery on the back of the bike, parking it by the entrance. When she saw where he was headed she waved him on, waiting by the gates. This was a private thing, something from his past that he had to lay to rest.

Jed walked over to Adrian's grave and looked down at the stone.

'After all we'd been through,' he said eventually, 'you shafted me, Adrian, you little shit!' He gave a shrug. 'But I forgive you, man. Rest easy.'

He walked away to where Wendy was waiting, back to where his roots were, where his inspiration came from and where his future lay.

JIMMY NAIL

CROCODILE
—SHOES—
II

THE NEW ALBUM OUT NOW
ON CD AND CASSETTE

INCLUDES 'COUNTRY BOY'
AND 'BLUE ROSES'

POCKET
B O O K S

SILENT WITNESS

A Doctor Samantha Ryan Mystery

Now a major TV series starring Amanda Burton

Nigel McCrery

When forensic pathologist, Dr. Sam Ryan, is
called out to a murder scene, she is far from
pleased. Tramping around a graveyard in the
dark is not how she'd planned to spend her day
off. And then another, related, death is
discovered, and Sam is under pressure to come up
with evidence the police desperately need. By
now, though, the killer has decided that Sam is a
threat and must be removed...

Silent Witness is the brilliant debut of a major
new talent in crime fiction - tautly written, it will
grip its readers right to its breathlessly tense
conclusion.

PRICE £4.99

ISBN 0 671 85506 9

POCKET
B O O K S

ORDER FORM

This book and other **Simon & Schuster** titles are available from your book shop or can be ordered direct from the publisher.

* Crocodile Shoes 0671 855824 £4.99
* Silent Witness 0671 855069 £4.99

Please send cheque or postal order for the value of the book, and add the following for postage and packing: UK inc. BFPO 75p per book; OVERSEAS Inc. EIRE £1 per book. OR: Please debit this amount from my:

VISA/ACCESS/MASTERCARD...

CARD NO...

EXPIRY DATE..

AMOUNT £...

NAME...

ADDRESS..

....

SIGNATURE..

Send orders to:
SIMON & SCHUSTER CASH SALES
PO Box 29, Douglas, Isle of Man, IM99 1BQ
Tel: 01624 675137, Fax 01624 670923
http://www.bookpost.co.uk
Please allow 28 days for delivery.
Prices and availability subject to change without notice.